Anita Hendy's

Father William

Anita Hendy ©

Published by
Anita Hendy
Prefix 0-9549641
Ballyteague Sth,
Kilmeague,
Naas,
Co. Kildare,
Ireland.

December 2006
2nd Edition.

No part of this publication may be reproduced, stored in a retrieval system, or transmitted in any form or by any means without the prior permission of the Publisher, or otherwise circulated in any form of binding or cover other than that which it is published and without a similar condition including this condition being imposed on the subsequent purchaser.

ISBN 0-9549641-5-2

Check out Anita's Web Site www.anitahendy.com

This book is the third part in a Trilogy
by Anita Hendy
The other two books are called
'A Girl Called Molly'
'The Furlong Spirit'

*'This 'Trilogy' is dedicated to
any reader whose lovely character
may have been hurt, & to whom Christian comfort
is weakened by the destructive influence of evil.
This 'Trilogy' was written so
that the grace of holiness may become a visible light
in all our eyes, giving love, forgiveness and peace
to the gentle hearts of all peoples in this beautiful world.'*

Anita Hendy 2006

Chapter 1.

A dense fog concealed much of the City of Dublin. Pierced only by the cone-shaped spires of the cathedrals and churches, its ghostly thick cloak descended on rich and poor alike. The homeless, lying on pavements and in doorways, pulled their cardboard blankets tightly around their cold bodies. Up above in the windows of the sleepy, bright lamps were reluctantly being switched on, their warm cozy glow serving only to make the homeless feel even more destitute and forgotten.

Then, with the approaching dawn, the early buses emerged from the depot belching black polluting smoke into the already stagnant air. It was through these almost eerie deserted streets that a brown Ford Cortina car drove carefully through the fog.

Suspended in the beam of its lights, the droplets of air danced and twirled to confuse the driver even more. Onwards it went, slowy winding its way towards Dublin Airport.

At the wheel of the car Fr. William Thornton strained his eyes to see. Flicking his headlights from full to dim, he was very thankful there was little traffic to contend with.

Beside him in the passenger seat, a young attractive girl of nineteen sat staring out of the car window. The pair had chatted for most of the way on their journey from Wexford, but then as they drew nearer to Dublin a quiet lull came over the conversation.

Molly Furlong began to think back over the last year.

She had passed her Leaving Certificate with honours and Auntie Hattie and all her family had been so pleased for her. Kate, her best friend, had done even better and was gone to a position in banking. As the girls left their school for the last time they had promised to keep in touch. However when the excitement died down, Molly found that she really did not know what career she wanted to follow. Aunt Hattie suggested, among other occupations, a secretarial course or teaching. But Molly felt that after being in boarding school for five years she needed some space and time on her own. She desperately wanted to recapture some of the freedom she had as a child. So after a little persuading, Aunt Hattie eventually agreed that she could stay home on the farm for a year.

However, like most people who go away for a time and then return, Molly found things to be not quite as they were.

The first thing she felt strange about was not returning to 'The Rectory', the house she felt was home. Auntie Hattie had moved in with her Grandad at 'Riversdale House'. Although she was very familiar with the house and loved her grandad dearly, Molly felt it was not the same. Her new bedroom held none of the dreams of her childhood.

Then there was Biddy. Since the maid was asked to leave 'Riversdale House', Molly found she really missed her company. She knew Biddy had given birth to a baby boy, Franks son, but the subject was never mentioned by any of the Furlong family.

Being a teenager, Molly could now explore more of the countryside. She would leave the house early and make towards the river. She discovered many more walks and trails, hills and dales. She always went alone and this gave her an exciting feeling of adventure. Instead of seeing a child running wildly across his fields, Walter Furlong was now seeing a young lady strolling thoughtfully through the wild flowers and green grass.

Being a passionate romantic, Molly had, throughout her puberty, fallen in love several times with some of the local boys. She loved dancing and was, at the drop of a hat, ready to travel to any of the discos around. But after the initial excitement and attraction of meeting a boy, she usually became bored with his company. Molly had a definite picture in her mind of the man who would capture her heart and deep down she knew she could not settle for less. But while wandering about, recapturing the wonder of her childhood, she also became aware of a slight seriousness creeping into her mind. She needed to look for and find herself.

Sometimes she would bring some paper with her and sketch a tree or landscape, other times she would return with a poem written from her heart. But all the time she found a peace and solitude almost as if she was being watched over by God Himself.

Now looking out of the car window she could see the lights of the Airport in the distance. Fr. William reached over and patted her hand reassuringly.

'The fog is lifting, it's not as bad out here,' he observed.

Relieved, she smiled back at him.

'Yes,' she thought to herself, 'I'm glad I spent that year at home.'

She began remembering back to when she had made up her mind to take up nursing as a career. It was the day her grandad, trying to choose a memoriam card for Aggie Cullen, handed her a bunch of keys and asked her to fetch some photographs from the old woman's cottage. Molly had been inclined too put off going to the cottage as it held too many memories. but as she walked across the fields these memories suddenly came flooding back. In the distance she could see the woods. She thought of all the times that Aggie had brought her there to gather sticks. Quickening her step she drew nearer to the cottage. She remembered the first day she had seen the hedge surrounding it and how high it seemed to be.

Since Aggie's death, Molly's grandad had the gate and door of the cottage locked up securely with two big iron chains and padlocks.

On reaching the small gate, she opened the lock and removed the chain. Then, lifting the bolt she walked slowly up the short path towards the brown wooden door. There were no cats to welcome her this time just some small birds resting on the old bench. They flew away quickly as she approached, exposing the old battered tin saucers lying around with which she used to feed Aggie's cats. Hesitating for a moment, she slipped the key into the lock and removed the chain. Lifting the latch, she opened the door slowly.

The deserted kitchen was in semi darkness as she looked sadly over at the cold hearth. Walking over to Aggie's chair a strange feeling came over her. She could feel Aggie's presence all around. Reaching out, she caressed the smooth black wood of her old armchair. In her mind's eye she could see Aggie sitting there. Suddenly her gaze fell on the stone floor. She imagined the old woman lying dead where her grandad told her he had found her. Shaking her head, she looked away in an effort to drive the awful thoughts from her mind. Then her gaze wandered around the room. Everything had been left just as it was when Aggie was alive. Nothing had been disturbed. All around, on ledges, chipped mugs and pots stood empty.

A heap of dusty old clothes covered the settle-bed in the corner. Molly wandered around touching and looking at everything. She remembered how big it had all seemed the first time she came there as a child. Now she could almost cross the kitchen floor with a couple of large steps.

The soldier still smiled his handsome smile from behind the brown glass in the framed photograph on the table. Although the familiar contents of the cottage were intact, Molly felt a lonely emptiness in the room.

Wandering over to the window, she looked out at the small overgrown garden. Her eyes took on the glazed expression of daydreamers. She began to finger the gold locket around her neck as little shivers of nostalgia crept up her spine.

She remembered the day she found the locket in the garden. Tears started in her eyes as she remembered Aggie's excitement when she showed it to her.

'Oh Aggie,' she sighed, 'I wish you were here. I need to talk to you. What am I to do with my life?'

But there was no reply, only the eerie sound of the wind rushing through a crack in the pane. Molly stood alone and in her loneliness, she felt she was being watched by an invisible friend. Large tears welled up in her eyes, and unable to hold them, they spilled over and trickled down her cheeks. Then she cried as only someone who feels the deep loss of a loved one can cry, her tears becoming an offering to God to bring Aggie back. After a little while she stopped crying and unhappily decided that there was nothing left in the cottage only memories.

Remembering the photographs, she went over to the dresser and opened a small drawer. Taking out a large thick envelope, she then closed the drawer and turned for the door.

In a few moments she had stepped out of the cottage, replaced the lock on the chain and sadly turned away.

As she went walking back down the path the heat of the sun's rays warmed and comforted her. Its bright rays shone on the wild flowers growing beside the path. As her eyes fell on the daisies and buttercups she smiled as she remembered the times she would pick those flowers and give them to Aggie.

'Yer a kind child,' Aggie would say tenderly, 'Ya give from yer heart. Someday ya'll give comfort to many without fear or thought of yerself.'

Suddenly Molly stopped. Looking around she instinctively felt the presence of an invisible friend. A great excitement came over her as she heard the words again.

'Could those people Aggie spoke about be the sick? Molly wondered.

By the time she had returned to Riversdale House she had made up her mind to take up nursing. Being too late with her application for that year to be accepted in any of the Irish hospitals, Auntie Hattie suggested they try the England instead. Then a month later, when Molly received word that she was accepted by Walton General in Liverpool, Aunt Hattie went ahead and made all the arrangements

'Look Molly we're almost there,' said Fr. William breaking into her thoughts and pointing ahead.

As they drove towards the car park Molly saw the lights of the main terminal building up ahead. They looked welcoming in the bleakness of the dark morning.

Stepping out of the warm car, a cold breeze blew sharply on their faces. Looking up, she could see the flashing light of a plane as it took off into the sky.

Opening the boot quickly, Fr. William took out a large suitcase while Molly lifted a smaller one. Then they hurried through the car park, across the tarmac and into the warmth of the main building.

After having the luggage and ticket checked in by a ground hostess, they then went upstairs to the restaurant. Being an hour early, they decided they had some time for a little breakfast. Molly went to the 'ladies' while William went to buy the food. By the time she returned he was already seated at a small table.

He watched her coming towards him across the room. Dressed in blue denim jeans and a jacket to match, she walked tall and smiling. The deportment lessons she learned in school were now very much in evidence. With her back held confidently erect, her long thick wavy black hair swung to the feminine movement of her body. The pure white young skin on her face was thankfully devoid of any make-up. Her big blue eyes smiled at him as she drew closer. He felt a lump rise in his throat. He remembered her christening, her first communion and confirmation. He remembered all the lovely times they shared when she was growing up. Now, as a teenager, she was on the verge of becoming a young woman.

The hot buttered toast and eggs tasted delicious and it was not long until William went to fetch another pot of tea.

Then over the loudspeaker passengers were asked to board the Liverpool flight, and it was time to leave. Reaching down, Molly picked up her small bag. Then pushing their chairs back they rose quickly from the table.

Watching her give her boarding card to the attendant, William knew she was about to leave Ireland for the first time. He whispered a silent prayer:

'God please keep her safe.'

Then she turned and, after giving him a hug, said sincerely:

'Thanks for everything, I'll write and tell you when I'm settled.'

There was so much he wanted to say to her like; 'keep your faith and your virtue' but looking into her pure blue eyes he decided to say nothing. Instead he put all his hope in the knowledge that the values she had been taught over the years, would now stand and guard her from any harmful influences that she might encounter.

'Goodbye child,' he said quietly, 'I'll pray for your success.'

Opening his arms, he suddenly felt as if he was letting a vulnerable bird fly from his hands. Then with another excited wave she disappeared around the corner. Fr. William stood alone. He did not want to return to the car just yet. He stepped out of the way of the other passengers saying goodbye to loved ones. Holding his arms tightly a strange feeling came over him. For a moment it was as if Molly's mother was standing beside him. Then a strange thought came into his mind. If things had worked out all those years ago, this could have been their daughter he was seeing off.

Looking out at the grey dawn, he became haunted by great feelings of loneliness. Once more he realised how much of the world he had given up for God. Eventually he turned and went down the stairs. Walking back towards the car he became a little anxious about Molly going away on her own. She would have been safer at home he thought.

Then looking up at the Aer Lingus plane climbing high in the sky, he knew that she was created for more.

Chapter 2.

With both hands Biddy Brown lifted a heavy bucket of water out of the sink and down onto the floor. Kneeling on a small mat, she took the scrubbing brush and dipped it into the water. Outside the back door her little son Danny slept peacefully in his pram. It was his first birthday today and Biddy could not help wondering if Frank, or any of the Furlong family would come to visit.

Reaching across the linoleum, she manoeuvred the brush into the little corners and crevices of the presses, the muscles of her back stretching as her body grew longer. Then, as her hand scrubbed in a circular movement, her mind began thinking back.

From the day her mother had brought her to work at Riversdale House she had never been happier. At first she was shy of the Furlong children, they were older, with a confidence about them. But as time went by she managed to hold her own with their tricks and their games.

David, the eldest, was the quiet one. If he was not working he could be found riding his horse Cuitteog across the fields. Doireann, the youngest and only girl, could switch from being like a kind sister one minute to a bossy boots the next.

But it was the boy in the middle, Frank, who captivated Biddy from the start. He helped her carry the heavy buckets of milk and would watch out for her safety when the cattle were around. In the evenings when all the work was done he would look across at her with a mischievous twinkle in his dark eyes. She would instantly respond and they would run about and play games in the farmyard, hiding in the sheds and ducking and weaving between the machinery. But as the years went by there came a day that would change all that innocent playfulness.

It was a warm summer's evening and they were both working in the cow house as usual. It was getting late and Biddy was tired. She was glad when Frank milked the last cow, untied it and hunted it out into the yard. As she bent down to lift the buckets of milk up off the ground she suddenly felt two strong arms encircle her waist.

'I have ya now, 'he said playfully as he held her in a tight grip.

He had often grabbed her like this but that night it felt different. They had both grown into young adults.

Suddenly a shy feeling went through her as she felt his body pressing just that little bit too close behind her. Dropping the buckets, she pressed both hands down on his arms.

'Frank stop yer messin'',' she pleaded as she wriggled to break free.

This wriggling seemed only to cause a greater excitement in Frank. Laughing, he wrestled to hold her even tighter. Panting and heaving, Biddy eventually managed to turn within his grasp. In a moment they were facing each other. He stood much taller at an inch off six feet. His thick coarse black hair hung long and wild around his face, and his wide mouth with large lips stretched into a very titillating grin.

She could feel his hot breath on her face. His eyes looked deep into hers. They had taken on a wild expression, that same look he would have racing a horse, or running through the meadows.

Suddenly Frank took a step back and stumbled. Together they fell backwards against the stone wall in the corner. The buttons of his shirt opened and Biddy could see the mass of black hairs on his chest. His dark skin's aroma mingled with the natural animal smell of the cow house and only added to the headiness of the moment.

Still holding her tight, Frank pressed his lips down hard on hers. Biddy did not know what to do. It was her first kiss. Then, just as quickly as he had grabbed her he let her go. Laughing, he ran out into the yard while Biddy stayed trembling in the corner. Holding her hand up to her tingling lips, she watched him drive the cows out of the yard towards the field. A thousand thoughts raced through her mind, most of them contradicting each other. The kiss had felt so strange. She never thought of Frank in this way. Maybe he was taking liberties with her affections and then again maybe he was not.

'Could he be in love with me?' she asked herself.

She did not know. But then nobody really knew Frank.

From then on little butterflies seemed to dance in her stomach whenever Frank was around. She would rise earlier in the morning to take more care with her appearance. Her lovely thick wild red hair now sported a satin ribbon. This ribbon was easily spotted blowing in the wind as she walked across the long meadow to work.

Having a four hundred acre farm at their disposal, the young lovers found great privacy and no shortage of hiding places in which to unleash their passion. They would often steal away in different directions only to meet up later at the same place. With Biddy forbidden by her mother to have any social life and Frank's work keeping him from the same, their little rendezvous held a mischievous excitement all of its own.

Once when they were in the throes of a passionate embrace Walter Furlong almost discovered them. Standing beneath the hay shed, he shouted a couple of times in different directions for Frank to join him. Far above his head, at the top of the bales of straw, the lovers lay quietly huddled together trying to cover their nakedness. They held their breaths hoping that he would go away. When after a few moments they heard him leave, they heaved great sighs of relief and collapsed into a childish laugh.

Biddy knelt up from the floor and paused from her chore. She smiled mischievously as she remembered that particular day.

Suddenly she heard her baby give a little cough in the pram outside the door. Wiping her hands in her apron, she went to go to him, but straining her ears to listen there was silence. So reaching for a cloth, she continued mopping up the water from the floor.

Suddenly the smile disappeared from her face when she thought about how her pregnancy had changed everything. Wringing the floor cloth out tightly she watched the clear sudsy water become dark and murky.

By the time she was aware of her pregnancy she was head over heels in love with Frank. She presumed he was with her. However, she would always remember his expression the day she told him about it.

His eyes darkened into blank pits of disappointment and fear. He took on the expression of a trapped animal.

In that moment Biddy felt so small. He had suddenly reduced her from being his equal to being his servant. She stood before him desperately hoping she misunderstood his look. She wanted him to embrace her, but instead he made a lame excuse and hurried off.

For days after he had avoided her. She grew lonely and angry. Then sheer frustration drove her to go and talk to the Boss. She thought he would understand because it was his grandchild she was carrying.

But the same Furlong cold stare told her she could expect nothing more from the Boss. Instead of words of comfort Walter told her she would have to leave. He would take care of everything and see it was provided for. Maybe a trust fund could be set up in the bank. Biddy barely heard his words. Tears of disbelief and abandonment welled up in her eyes as she turned and fled from the room.

Meeting Doireann at the kitchen door, she was unable to stop but ran hysterically past her. She never returned to Riversdale House again. Remembering that time now, a horrible feeling suddenly came over her and she shivered.

With her temper rising she wiped her perspiring brow with her apron. Then, dipping the brush once again deep into the dirty water, a small evil voice taunted her mind.

'This is your height now Biddy Brown, scrubbing floors. Serves ya right, ya thought ya could be better than the rest. Ya thought ya could live in the big house, your so stupid.'

To block out what she thought were her own depressing thoughts, she began scrubbing the floor more vigorously.

Once again the isolation and pain of her son's birth flashed before her eyes. At least Doireann could have come to visit her in the hospital. She had wanted her to come. But in the end nobody came, no friends and no family. There was just Biddy and her baby.

Having finished cleaning the floor she got up off her knees and walked to the back door. With great force she emptied the contents of the bucket out into the yard. She watched as the wet dirty water spread finger like over the dry white cement and branching out into little channels.

Drying her eyes with her apron, she took a deep breath. She looked proudly into the pram to check if her son was still sleeping.

'Well,' she thought hopefully, 'that's all in the past now. Everyone was upset then. Things are different now. This healthy baby is Frank's son, Walter's first grandson. Sure they'd have ta come today, I know they will. They will love the child when they see how beautiful he is.'

Then, with these stubborn thoughts of hope building up in her mind she stared out across the green meadow.

Up at Riverdale House the Furlong men worked on as usual. They were unaware that across their fields, a young woman's heart was almost bursting with longing.

Chapter 3.

It was a year now since Hattie Thornton had moved in to live with her brother at Riversdale House.

With her sister-in-law's early death, and her niece Doireann's disinterest over the years, she found that the house had undergone little change since her childhood. Doireann had just recently married Garrett O'Loughlin and moved to a stud farm in Co.Longford.

Hattie, having sold her own house and most of its contents, brought only a few treasured and personal possessions with her. Like her favourite wedding present, a tea set of china, her French bed and her Piggott piano. These few antique pieces blended in perfectly with the style of furniture already there and she took a lot of comfort from being surrounded by the familiar things of her childhood.

At first she found it very strange to be back in the old house. It seemed to her that her life had come full circle. If it was not for her reflection in the mirror, and a few aches and pains in her joints, she might well believe she was a child again.

It did not take long for Walter to realise that his sister had arrived. That first morning when he had finished milking, his eyebrows lifted in surprise as he walked into the kitchen for his breakfast. An immaculate white linen cloth was spread over the long table. A glass vase of colourful fresh flowers stood in the centre. Delicate china cups and crockery were placed with perfection at each table setting. Frank was already seated with his dark muscular arms folded and a huge grin all over his face. Pulling out his chair, Walter fingered a matching napkin folded neatly in a silver serviette ring on his side plate.

He rested his chin amusedly on his joined hands as he watched Hattie take some freshly baked bread from the oven.

He said hopefully, 'I hope the cookin' has improved since the old days.'

He began remembering how their mother, God rest her, would say in a voice of desperation, that his sister would have to marry a rich man because she was hopeless on the domestic front.

He had to stifle a laugh when he thought of what Aggie Cullen would think about it all if she were alive now. But then his face took on a more serious expression as Hattie turned and carried their breakfasts over to the table.

The rashers were a little overdone, and the eggs were hard, but the bread was warm and tasty and the tea was good and strong, just as he liked it.

'This is all very nice,' said Walter tactfully, 'but if ya don't mind I'd prefer to drink out of me auld mug.'

Hattie quickly obliged and within minutes had taken a blue willow patterned mug from the dresser and sat it on the china saucer.

From then on there was an unspoken understanding that while some things were not to be changed, others could easily be worked out by compromise. Walter and Frank were only too glad to let Hattie take over the running of the house.

Dressed in a frilly apron, with her cigarettes and lighter in the pocket, she set about putting her own unique style and touches to every room. But while working she found she had almost too much time to think.

Memories of the wonderful romantic months she had with Nicholas Robinson came back to her. Pausing from her work, she would gaze out the windows across the fields. She carried those memories like a child carrying a little box of secret treasures. She could not share them with anyone. They were so precious. Only when she was alone could she open her heart and take them out. Then she would ponder and caress each thought lovingly. She wondered where he was now and what he was doing. She wondered if he ever thought of her. Like anyone who had heart and soul passionately lifted from this world by a romance, Hattie had found it hard to come back to reality. Her body moved automatically while her mind was locked into the past.

She remembered how for days after he had gone she had shut herself up in the Rectory and contacted no one.

At first the immense loss of Nicholas's company opened a great void of loneliness. Then, into this open and vulnerable wound, a deep agonizing pain took root and began to eat into her very being. Her body could find no rest and her sleep when it eventually found her, was very disturbed. She would constantly sink deep into continuous nightmares. Then memories of her young days would lift her up to happier times, but on wakening up again, her unhappiness was so great she would sink back into despair again. In the middle of all this tossing and turning, she would clutch her arms tightly and rock, and cry bitterly. Then all cried out she would sit up in bed again, and with her eyes registering a blank expression, she would stare at nothing in particular. Pulling hard on her cigarettes to give her relief, the deadly weeds were her only comfort and seemed lately to give little relief. As time went by she was unaware of how quickly the ashtray was filing up with butts. For a long time she had remained in this terrible state. Wallowing in self pity, she began to lose her appetite and her usual groomed appearance. One day went by as slowly as the next and as they did, she became thoroughly exhausted. falling further down into a dark pit of despair, Hattie had almost given up on herself.

Now, two months later, as she dusted the window ledges, she stopped suddenly as she remembered how then in her misery she thought she had heard a voice, saying:

'Do not be afraid, I am with you even to the end of time.'

Hattie had stayed very still. Did she really hear it or was it something she already knew. Hoping the voice would speak again she had cried softly:

'Don't leave me Lord I am your child, gather me in your arms and hold me close, I need you.'

That one small prayer, spoken with tears of sincerity, like a ray of light penetrated the black darkness. Suddenly a great calm had come over her and peace had once more entered her soul. She got up slowly from the bed and walked towards the window.

Now she had a great need to let light in. Pulling the curtains back she remembered how the brightness of the sun had stung her heavy eyes. Then, as she opened the window, the scent of the summer flowers drifted up from below.

Hattie inhaled deeply and it was in that moment she knew she had come back to reality. From then on she had kept herself busy each day with the task of selling her house. Finding it hard to make quick decisions, she dithered and pondered whether to sell her furniture or not. In the end Walter convinced her that neither of them had any need for it.

In the weeks that followed she put all thoughts of Nicholas away once more in that place in her heart, and closed the lid on her box of memories. From then on she became emotionally stronger and resumed her usual air of confidence.

As she put her duster away Hattie Thornton decided that if she was going to make a sacrifice, she would do it, not with a sad face but with a twinkle in her eyes and a smile on her lips.

There was only one person who would have known what was behind that smile and that man was Nicholas Harrison.

CHAPTER 4.

Eithne Thornton took one more deep breath. Having gone beyond the point of endurance she gripped her hands into a tight fist. Her lovely thick hair hung wet and limp around her hot flushed face. Large beads of perspiration trickled down her heaving body.

'Come now dear, you must push harder,' said the midwife in an anxious voice at the end of the labour table.

Eithne looked up at the clock on the wall. It had been yesterday evening when she felt the first pains of birth. Now, four hours later, she wondered if this time she would surely die. Then, with an enormous will to live she breathed in and pushed down.

'I'm afraid we will have to help this baby along,' said the midwife, taking a large scissors from a metal tray.

Eithne was in such distress that she did not care what happened as long as somebody stopped the dreadful pain.

'Oh,' she thought anxiously, 'where's Seamus? I want him here with me.'

Her husband, Dr. Thornton, had been with her up to an hour ago but then he suddenly left.

After making a small incision in Eithne's body the midwife stood waiting. With the next pain her patients whole being seemed to contract. Her face screwed up in agony and her breath almost stopped in her chest.

Submissively, she bowed her head and gave in to a power greater than she. Her hand reached out desperately for something to hold and the young nurse took it quickly. The force of the enormous push caused a little head of black hair to appear between her thighs, its tiny face covered in blood and its eyes closed.

'Well done dear,' said the delighted midwife as she supported the little head turning in her hand.

Rising up on her elbows, Eithne tried to see over her large bump but could see very little.

'Just one more push now pet,' said the midwife encouragingly.

Her patient lay back exhausted.

Looking up at the ceiling, she knew that her labour would be over soon. Then within minutes the powerful muscles of her womb, like two giant clamps, closed in and sent a severe agonizing pain right through her. As the baby's body slid through the bones of her pelvis, her body felt as if it was being torn apart. An animal like groan escaped from her dry lips.

Relieved to see the baby delivered safely at last the midwife called out excitedly as she clamped and cut the cord:

'It's a little boy,'

A young student nurse looked on in amazement as she wiped Eithne's forehead with a cool wet cloth. The baby, on entering the world let out a loud screeching cry. Tears of relief ran down its mothers face as her body trembled with the tremendous shock of the birth.

'Is he alright?' she asked worriedly.

Running her eyes over his tiny body, the nurse did a quick examination including counting fingers and toes,

'He seems perfect,' she said as she lifted him up and laid the baby's warm wet body on his mothers chest.

The pain of the last few hours was momentarily forgotten in the joy of holding him close. His little body was covered all over by a white cream like substance. Eithne pressed her nose to his soft head and smelt the wonderful aroma of new birth. Suddenly his little eyes opened and with a great serious expression far exceeding his age, he stared at his mother. In that fleeting moment Eithne beheld his soul. This was the bond that confirmed for all time that he was hers.

'I will love you forever,' she whispered as she bent her head and lovingly kissed the gift that God had given her. Then the midwife gently took him away to attended to his needs.

Eithne lay back exhausted. The sudden shock caused by the expulsion of the baby from her body caused her to shake uncontrollably. Soaked with her blood, the sheet felt cold and wet beneath her. Noticing this, the student nurse fetched another green blanket, covered and tucked it warmly around her.

Eithne placed her hand on her abdomen. After being swollen for nine months with the baby it now felt soft, empty and flabby.

'I'm afraid you will need some stitches down here,' said the nurse as she removed the afterbirth and examined her.

'Nothing to worry about though, the doctor will be here in a few minutes.'

But Eithne was worried. Once again she prayed that the Doctor who would repair the damage of birth, would be gentle, capable and preferably old.

A little while later, with the dreaded procedure over, she was wheeled on a trolley up the long corridors and into a private room. Then she was helped into bed and given a cup of tea. Beside her in a plastic crib, lay her ten pounds baby sleeping peacefully.

She raised the cup to her lips and closed her eyes in ecstasy. The sheer pleasure of swallowing that first mouthful of tea was written all over her face. But it was not until she had relished two more cups that her great thirst was truly satisfied.

Then she placed the cup on the locker and lay back on the pillows. God it was like the calm after the storm.

Although she felt sore and tender the relief of having no more severe pain was overwhelming. Her body was exhausted but her mind was racing. Looking at the sleeping baby in his cot she smiled. Then reaching over, she slipped her index finger into his tiny hand.

In that moment no jewels, no possessions, nothing the world had to offer could give the joy that she beheld. It almost pulled her heart out from her breast. She felt a fulfilment that surpassed all understanding. Once again giving birth had instilled in her soul a spiritual unspoken commitment. This could only be carried out with extreme bravery. No pain was too much to bear for it, no sacrifice too great to save it. By forgetting herself she would become its protector, its nurturer, its teacher and its friend. Once more she had been given a glimpse of what it was like to be a creator, and in doing so graciously honoured her deserving title of mother.

By the time Dr. Thornton returned his fifth child had entered the world. He also secretly hoped that this might be the last one. Not that he did not love his children, of course he did, no, what he wanted now more than anything else was to get back the girl he had fallen in love with before they came.

How many times had he gone home tired after an exhausting day at the hospital thinking about the evening ahead.

He always fantasized that Eithne would be waiting for him when he returned home. Maybe she would be wearing something to please and him. He needed to make love to her. This was his way of expressing his love for her.

She had been there for him in the beginning of their marriage, but with the birth of each child those precious times got less. How often had he been disappointed, on arriving home, when he found her nursing or attending to the children's needs. He began to notice how her figure had never regained its youthful shape. Instead of dressing in smart cut clothes she seemed to favour sloppy comfortable ones. In fact some of the time he could get a faint smell of baby sick from them too.

Lately he began to notice other women flirting with him at the hospital or in the street. By their dress, their smile or their movements they would always manage to catch his eye. Instinctively he would smile back. Although they attracted and stirred a boyish excitement in him, he knew deep down that their eyes did not hold the sincerity that he saw in his wife's.

However, over the years feelings of rejection began creeping into his mind and he tried hard not to dwell on them. He seemed to be very much on the outside of what seemed to be a little circle of Eithne and the children. Unable to talk to his wife about these feelings, more destructive thoughts took root. Then before long he found that they had taken a firm hold.

He began to think foolishly that all his wife needed him for was to make babies. Once that was done it seemed he was pushed into the background again. Most of the time she seemed to reject his passion, with excuses that she was too sick or too tired. Once a week they might make love if he was lucky, and then it was more a case of she letting him than joining him.

Housework and décor suddenly became so important. It seemed as if there was always something new to buy. The groceries, the house repairs and the bills were endless. In desperation he had suggested to her that she go see a colleague of his about contraception. But she had refused. Without giving him a reason he immediately presumed it was the ultimate rejection.

So, as Dr. Seamus Thornton drew nearer to Holles St. Hospital and his wife Eithne, he secretly hoped that maybe this time, things would be different.

CHAPTER 5.

'Are ya alright geill?' said the fat bald taxi driver in his best scouse accent. Bending down he picked up Molly's large suitcase and put it in the front of his cab. Climbing in the back with the small one, Molly realized to her amazement that she could not understand his Scouse accent.

'Sorry what did you say?' she asked confusedly.

'Where to?' he said, hopping into the front and adjusting the meter.

'Walton Hospital please.'

'Okay luv,' came the reply, as the driver turned the key in the ignition and started the engine.

Driving out of Speke Airport, Molly found it hard to believe she was in England. The journey from Dublin had taken a little over half an hour. The Aer Lingus plane she had travelled on had been both exciting and scary. With a seat belt securely fastened around her, Molly had braced herself for take off.

The speed of the aircraft was thrilling, but once airborne she looked out the window and suddenly became aware of how frighteningly high she was flying.

Then she watched the plane fly through a lot of misty dark cloud. But once above it, nothing could have prepared her for the scene that met her eyes. Like flames of vivid red fire, the rising sun spread a golden glow across the top of an endless sea of cotton wool.

Striking rays of bright light created great masses of colour. The whole sky shimmered as they passengers flew towards the sun. Everywhere Molly looked different shapes of horse's birds and angels seemed to appear in the clouds. But as soon as these images were formed they disappeared again. At one time she even imagined she saw the face of God.

She wondered what it would be like to step out of the plane and dance among the clouds. She would have loved to feel the fluffiness beneath her feet and the weightlessness of space around her limbs.

'Come from Paddyland have ya geill?' said the taxi driver, breaking into her thoughts.

Molly did not understand.

Getting no reply to his question he explained,

'All you Irish are called Paddy's didn't ya know that?'

Embarrassed, Molly gave a little laugh but she did not think it was funny. Suddenly she became aware that she was not in her own country.

Driving through the City of Liverpool she could not help but admire the old impressive stone buildings. But it was the shops that really caught her attention. At last she would be able to buy all the lovely clothes she had seen in the magazines at home. Although it was scary being in this big city all on her own, Molly felt very grown up too.

Deciding it would be better not to enter into conversation with the taxi driver she remained quiet for the rest of the half hour journey.

When they eventually pulled up at hospital Molly asked to be let out at the main door. Having paid the fare, she struggled with her cases up the steps. Once inside the entrance, she inquired from the young girl at the reception desk as to where she should go. Picking up a telephone receiver the girl made a quick call and in a few minutes a very neat, thin, efficient looking woman walked briskly through the swing doors.

'Hello there,' she said extending her hand cheerfully towards Molly,

'I'm Mrs. Woods, one of your tutors. I'll take you over to Hill House, the nurses home.'

Molly was delighted to hear her Irish accent. Accepting her friendly handshake Molly introduced herself in return.

Walking back out again through the main door she was amazed at how big the hospital grounds were. Commenting on this Mrs. Woods replied,

'Walton is one of the largest and best training hospitals in Liverpool and it is the only one with a brain surgery unit. See that flat roof up there?' she said pointing to a smaller building.

'That is where the helicopters land. We have a prison just up the road and, of course, Aintree racecourse is close by. Now don't worry, there are lots of Irish girls here and it won't take you long to find your way around.'

When they arrived at the nurses quarters seemed almost as big as the hospital itself. Molly's room was on the ground floor and down a long corridor. Mrs. Woods unlocked the door and handed her the key.

'Now dear,' she said, entering the room, 'male visitors are not allowed stay overnight and you must keep this door locked at all times. The cleaners come in every second day but they have there own key. Leave your cases down there and I'll show you the rest of the place.'

Curiously, Molly followed her into a large bare kitchen, a communal sitting room, three old white-tiled bathrooms, the laundry room and another recreational room. One had table tennis and a piano in it. Then they arrived back to the main hall again. Pointing to some tickets on a little table, her guide said, smiling:

'The nightclubs in town provide free passes for the nurses so you will be able to have some fun. The warden locks the main door of the home at 11 o clock and after that you will have to ring a bell to gain entry.'

Then, smiling, her escort handed her a timetable and a book of instructions.

'I will see you in class at nine sharp in the morning Nurse Furlong and I expect nothing from you but your best. Somehow I don't think I will be disappointed.'

Molly thanked her and said goodbye. She felt quite chuffed at unexpectedly being called Nurse. Then, picking up a selection of tickets from the small table, she studied them excitedly as she walked back to her room.

Sitting on the small bed, she looked around. The ceiling was very high but the room was small and narrow. There were only two bits of furniture in it, a very plain wardrobe and dressing table. Beside the dressing table was a notice board. A small sink stood in the corner beside the large Georgian window. Familiar cold feelings of the discipline of boarding school came flooding back to her. Standing up she wandered over to the window. She looked out at the tall hospital buildings across the grounds. There was not a blade of grass in sight.

Then in her mind she heard words Aggie Cullen said to her many years ago.

'From now on child yer days of freedom will be less. Guard yer heart and thoughts if ya want to keep them. Carry with ya memories of yer childhood and don't let things disturb ya.'

Tears welled up in her eyes as a lump caught in her throat.

'Oh Aggie,' she cried.

Placing her hands on the window, she pressed her head sadly against the glass. In that moment an overwhelming yearning for home clutched at her heart.

Chapter 6.

It was now almost a month since Fr. William had left Molly at Dublin Airport. Sitting at his desk in the presbytery in County Laois, he was delighted when he received the usual monthly letter from her. Reclining back in his oak chair he was pleased to read that she had passed most of her exams in made lots of friends. The letter was short but held great promises of longer ones to follow. So, with a rather relieved smile on his face, William replaced the letter back in its envelope and slipped it into his pocket.

Sitting in deep thought for a few moments, he then rose from his chair and walked slowly over towards the window. His gaze took on a far away expression as he looked out thoughtfully through the small panes of glass. Then he began thinking about his own life.

Standing with his hands clasped at his waist, he thought of his achievements to date and his hopes for the future. Being honest in his thinking he knew that, since the building of the new church a few years ago, he had achieved nothing. In a strange way it seemed his parishioners were starting to take him for granted. This hurt William a little, but he bravely reminded himself that after all he had come to serve them.

Then his eyes roamed over the gloomy landscape. He could not help feeling that there must be something more, something deeper to life that he had not experienced yet. He never tired of reading and searching for it especially when he was ministering to the sick and dying. In his natural ability to serve, he brought through real sincerity, the peace that only comes from God to people in grief. Leaning forward he placed his hands on the window ledge, and looked down at the floor.

Now at forty-four years of age, he still had a strong enthusiasm for his parish and this was backed up by his unshakeable faith.

Lately, however, small fears had begun to creep into his mind as to the way things seemed to be heading. The same parishioners, with preconceived ideas about how the parish should be run, were turning up at the meetings.

Although these were good people and they meant well, unlike the priests, they had no training in spirituality. Their thinking leaned very much towards the world. William knew he could always depend on them to run functions and to fundraise etc. but when it came to making decisions of the church, it seemed to William he was in great need of a religious.

'But then,' he thought to himself, 'doesn't the Bishop like well oiled dioceses and parishes that are working properly?'

Even the young men coming out of the seminaries and colleges these days tended to be more organisational. Then doubts began to creep in that maybe he should lighten up a little and move with the times.

Still, as he turned from the window all this still played on his mind.

The hopes and aspirations of his vocation all those years ago seemed now to be locked in a legal system. After all that time he found the Bishops relationship was still very much authority and obedience. This, William felt, stopped him from achieving his true potential. In fact he now feared that with another change of Bishop, would come a change of dioceses.

Suddenly he heard Fr. Breens heavy footsteps on the stairs. William walked over to the door. On opening it he watched his parish priest descend the last wide step and walk hurriedly towards the ebony hallstand.

'Have to rush or I'll be late for this wedding,' he said anxiously.

William walked over towards the ebony hallstand. As Fr. Breen took up his umbrella, William took the heavy black coat down from the hook and held it while the older man slipped his arms into it.

'Thank you Willie, I'll see you at lunch,' he said gratefully as he checked his car keys and hurried out the front door.

William walked to the door and smiled as he watched him hurry to get into his little grey Toyota car. Then, accelerating noisily around the circular flowerbed in the centre of the front yard, he drove off quickly down the winding avenue. As the dust settled, the younger priest stood at the door looking out across the fields.

He started to think about Fr. Breen and began comparing himself to the latter.

Since the parish priest moved into the same house with William some months ago, William found their long and lengthy discussions were both beneficial and enlightening. Concerning some of the parish projects Fr. Breen would allow William to go so far but no further.

Although this caused some disagreements, William always respected his superior's decision. He actually found a quiet strength in Fr. Breens personality. But while listening to him, one thing constantly bothered William, Fr. Breen seemed to have a blind spot, an almost hardheartedness in his attitude.

He stubbornly seemed to be in no doubt about what was right and what was wrong. In fact he seemed to be, in William's opinion, completely black and white. Sometimes people would call to the Presbytery with problems and Fr. Breen, having listened to them, would make a decision and leave it at that. However, William found that he could not do this so readily. He often delayed making his decision, preferring to discuss their problems further at another time.

In his pondering about this, William felt that although Fr. Breens decisions were quite sensible, they seemed to be delivered with almost no compassion. This lack of compassion caused William to think that his parish priest was only partly right in his judgements. In many a situation William tried to bridge the gap between the heart and the head.

He never tired of reading and searching for answers. This searching was expressed mostly through his administration to the sick and dying. In his willingness to serve, he brought, through real sincerity, the peace of God to people in grief.

He was proud of his background and his education. His brother, Seamus Thornton, was now a consultant in the medical profession and a good family man. His mother, Hattie, over the last year had proved, by her enormous sacrifice concerning Nicholas Robinson, the good and honourable people he had come from. Oh yes, William was very proud of his family.

Suddenly the sky darkened overhead and a heavy shower of rain began to fall. Stepping inside, and closed the front door. But as Fr. William walked back down the hall, little did he know then, that before the next three years were out, his own courage, humility and faith would be tested in a way that would make even the angels tremble.

Chapter 7.

'David, there's a lovely house for sale in Bray,' said Alishe Furlong to her husband trying hard not to sound too excited.

It had been a while since she had visited 'Riversdale House' and David was surprised when he saw her car drive up the avenue earlier that evening.

'We can't afford it,' her husband quietly replied.

Sitting comfortably at the fire in the sitting room she ignored his remark and continued,

'The house is two-storey with a wonderful view and a beautiful garden. We can have barbecues in summer and we won't have to live over my office anymore. Darling it's going to make such a difference to our lives.'

From behind the newspaper came the same reply:

'Alishe, I said we can't afford it.'

At this repeated statement a small twinge of annoyance rose up inside her. Standing up, she suppressed her disappointment and walked over to the mantelpiece. Straightening one of the Belleek ornaments, she continued:

'I was speaking to the auctioneers and they have somebody interested in that old fish shop.'

'Oh yes,' muttered David.

Calculatingly she walked over beside him and sat down on the arm of his chair. Slipping her arm affectionately around his shoulders she caressed the back of his head.

'These people interested in the shop, are they friends of yours?' he asked curiously as he turned a page.

'Don't be silly darling, undertakers actually.'

Dropping the newspaper with both hands, David looked up angrily at his wife.

'How insensitive can you be.'

'But it's been sitting there idle now for the last year,' she protested, trying to calm him.

'We could do so much with the money. Oh David this is our chance to have a real home together.'

With the paper now crumpled in his right hand, David stood up from his chair.

'Oh no you won't get around me that way, you know I'll never sell the place.'

In the silence that followed, Alishe decided to make one last plea for her case.

Walking over to David, she put her arms around his neck and looked up affectionately into his eyes. Her voice softened to almost a purr:

'But darling, in this house in Bray,' she explained, 'we'll have a home for our children. Somewhere safe, where the air is fresh and the people are nice.'

David looked down at his wife, how well he knew her tactics. She would say anything to get her own way. In the heady days when they were locked in the first flushes of romance he would have fallen for it. But over the last few years he had come to know his second wife very well. She was an ambitious determined young woman.

Reaching up, he took her arms down firmly from his neck and stepped to the side.

'You told me it would be years before you would want children.'

Then, shaking his head, he continued:

'No I can't believe you now. You just want to entertain your yuppie friends. That house would be full of strangers.'

Clenching her fists tightly, her long painted nails dug sharply into her palms as she tried to stay calm.

'Look, don't be stupid it makes sense to sell that shop. I know you would like to keep it for Molly but you must let the past go. There is no guarantee that she would want to live in that street anyway. In the meantime it's just sitting there.'

Taking a step away from her, David said smugly:

'Well it so happens I have other plans for it now. I have been thinking quite a lot lately and Matty and I have decided to go into business. We are going to open the shop.'

Alishe's eyes widened in utter surprise;

'But what would you sell?' she asked with a slight chuckle.

'Electrical appliances,' he replied proudly.

Alishe suddenly broke out into a sarcastic laugh and sat down in the armchair.

'Oh dear, could you not think of something better to sell than that,' she asked as she examined her nails.

'Anyway what about your work on the farm?'

'Don't worry leave that to me.'

It was bad enough, that her little performance did not get the expected results, but when she realised David had made plans without consulting her, her anger could no longer be concealed.

'Well what about us then?'

'What about us?' he answered matter of fact.

Rising from her chair, her eyes darkened.

'Now you listen to me David, I've worked very hard in the last few years. I am just about to be accepted into that elite and closed circle of the Law Society. I feel I deserve your support in this matter. We can have it all.'

Listening to his wife, David could not believe what he was hearing.

'What the hell are you talkin' about. This bloody circle, who are these people? What have they to do with you and me?'

A look of pride flashed across her face as her voice rose to a crescendo:

'Oh you are so stupid, don't you realise that they have become part of my life. Have you been so caught up in the muck down here that you cannot see the sophistication and intelligence that they have brought into our lives? I have earned their respect admiration and comradeship. I am invited to the best restaurants and houses in Dublin. These people know how to make a success of their lives. For God sake David they are our friends.'

Although she was standing only a few feet from him, David felt, on hearing her words, that the space between them was as great as the wall of china. Suddenly he had a great need to get out of the house and into the fresh air.

Walking towards the door, he turned back as his hand twisted the knob.

'There may be muck down here,' he said with his dark eyes flashing, 'but at the end of the day it can always be washed off.'

Chapter 8.

Walter and Frank Furlong sat quietly in the kitchen of Riversdale House.

Hattie, his sister had gone to Mount Benedict to visit Lady Gowne for the evening.

A large cardboard box stood in the centre of the table and spread right across it were tax returns, receipts, forms from the marts, co-ops, the grain intake, the meat factories, the sugar company etc. In fact there were forms of every description. Picking up yet another one, Frank scratched his head and looked down confusedly at it.

Having left school at the age of twelve, he always thought that if he could count sheep and read comics he was educated. But it was only times like this that he would admit to himself that his education was definitely limited. All these forms were very worrying.

'What the hell is Domestic Outgoings?' he asked confusedly.

Walter reached over and took the blue form from his son. Holding the piece of paper at arm's length he adjusted his glasses. After studying it carefully for a few moments he did not want to admit that he couldn't understand any of it so he just threw it into the box with the others.

'Look son, its goin' to take smarter men than us to fill in all this.' he said wisely.

Rising from his chair, he walked out of the kitchen and into the hall. When he returned he had a bottle of Jameson whisky in one hand and two glasses in the other.

'Gather up them papers there now,' he said motioning to the table, 'I've had enough of that for this day.'

As Frank gathered the papers up one form in particular caught his attention. Picking it up he looked up worriedly at his father.

'Ya know boss the world is changin'. This one here says it has to be filled in if you want to retire. It's all about inheritance. I think.'

Walter put the bottle of whiskey down firmly on the table. His usual calm eyes took on an angry expression as he looked across at Frank.

'Ah will ya put it away will ya.' he said crossly,' When I retire son I'll be wearin' a wooden overcoat and I can assure ya I won't be liven on no hand outs from the Government. It's bad enough that they humiliate us with their forms and their subsidies, but if they had lived up to their promises we wouldn't have to be at this, this evenin.'

Sitting down on his chair again he unscrewed the bottle of whisky and poured out two drinks. Then with the tops of his fingers, he pushed one over towards Frank. Taking a fair sip of his own, Walter swallowed, and as his mouth savoured the bite of its fire, his cheeks sucked in with great satisfaction. Sitting back a little more relaxed now he began reminiscing.

'Do you remember? 'he asked Frank as he rolled the glass between his big hands,' when the politicians were goin' round campaignin' 'for us to join the EEC. They promised us then that they'd be able to market everythin' that we produced. But instead of keepin' those promises what did they do? I'll tell ya what they did, they brought in quotas on this, restrictions on that, subsidies on the other and penalties on producing too much. Son, somebody's made a right mess of somethin' and I'll tell ya now it's not the farmer.'

Walter took another sip of his drink and then replaced the glass on the table.

'Tell me where do ya see this farm goin' son?' he asked seriously as he leaned forward on the table and stared Frank between the two eyes.

Frank twisted his glass nervously between his rough hands. Then, looking right back at his father, he answered confidently:

'I tell ya one thing if everyone worked as long and hard, and had the dedication and commitment of the farmers of Wexford this 'id be one hell of a country.'

Walter's old tanned face broke out in a broad smile. He was very pleased with his son's reply. Picking up his glass again he reached over and tipped it off Frank's. The room rang to a musical clink of the crystal.

'Well, whatever about the country,' said Walter sincerely, 'I hope this place will always be in good hands.'

Putting the cap back on the bottle, he took the whisky up and walked back out into the hall. After replacing it carefully in the sideboard in the sitting room, he returned to the kitchen. Then he picked up his old cap from the cooker rail and turned to Frank.

'Go into Carnew early tomorrow and find a good accountant to look after them forms will ya son?'

Frank, sitting quite relaxed and sipping his whiskey happily replied:

'Okay boss, will do.'

With a sigh of relief Walter pulled the cap down on his head, picked up his stick and walked out into his yard.

'Oh God,' he thought to himself, 'How them people work in offices I'll never know.'

Whistling for his faithful companion, his sheep dog appeared at his side within minutes. Then, as they had often done before, they wandered off together in the direction of the high fields.

The vast autumn sky stretching before them appeared as a wall of flame. As if sketched by the hand of a master, the branches of the tall dark trees stood out boldly against the red flame like glow of the setting sun. In between, the brilliant light broke through, flashing a diamond. Like a thousand beggars, the branches rustled their leaves imploring mother nature not to strip them of the little they had. And with its own silent power, the earth took the noise of the day and wound it down to a peaceful stop.

It was while walking through this welcome stillness that Walter wondered about his children.

Doireann, his only daughter was happy and contented. Her marriage to Garrett O' Loughlin seemed to bring a happy end to a very restless youth. But it had taken a long time for her to find her way. There were times in the past when Walter just could not cope with her moods, and sought refuge in the outdoors.

David, on the other hand had his mother's restless spirit, and although he tried, it did not lend itself to the rural way of life. Walter had no problem with David's first marriage to Molly, God rest her, but he found it hard to accept his second wife with Alishe. These modern type marriages were really beyond his understanding. In his day a couple lived together all the time.

Then there was Frank. He, more than any of his children, had a true feeling for the land. But after that dreadful episode with Biddy he worried about his lack of socialising. Frank kept himself to himself and was definitely a one man farmer.

Reaching the top field, Walter looked out across his beloved farm.

'You know what Shep,' he said, as the dog rubbed against his trousers.

'When my time comes to pass on, I think the farm would be in good hands if I left it to Frank, what do ya say?'

As if in total agreement, Shep let out a loud bark and then the two friends turned for home.

Chapter 9.

It was now six months since Molly had started nursing in Liverpool. Having completed the first eight weeks in the classroom, she was now enjoying her practical work on the ward. Receiving ninety pounds in a monthly wage, she found it very hard to budget, as each month seemed a very long one.

The week before payday was particularly long. In the nurses home beans on toast were shared around like gold, and cornflakes saved many a hungry student from fainting.

But as time went by Molly and her friends learned how to manage their wages a little better. With a small amount put by in a building society, they would climb excitedly into the black hackney taxis and go shopping in Liverpool with the rest. Molly loved to explore the wonderful shops of the city and never tired of the creative stylish English fashion.

At the weekends Hill House nurses home hummed to pop music blaring out from radios. Girls hurried in and out of each other's room's borrowing makeup and clothes. Long queues formed for the bathrooms and the telephones in the hall were never free.

But it was the powerful magic of the city at night that excited Molly most. Wonderful mouth-watering aromas drifted teasingly from Chinese, Greek and Indian restaurants while others, with their neon signs flashing, tried to entice her inside. After the dull hospital canteen food all month, the restaurant dishes looked and smelled delicious. Molly and her friends relished each mouthful of spicy kebabs and hot curry's.

Afterwards, as they strolled along the streets, 'wine bars' packed tightly with young people just begged to be entered, while the many nightclubs, with the lively beat of their pop music, was all they needed to let their hair down.

However, for all their high-spiritedness and carefree ways, once the students were back in their nurses uniform and on the wards, they took their vocation very seriously. Young girls and boys, of many nationalities, lifted people twice their size in an effort to make them more comfortable. They bathed and washed strangers as if they were their own. They held tin vessels of various shapes while patients relieved themselves of their dreadful pain. They comforted children, reassured mothers, calmed men and fed the elderly and handicapped. They brought tiny new lives into the world and, with great dignity and compassion, helped others to leave it. They gave up weekends, bank holidays and Christmas's and worked hard on unsociable shifts. In doing all this they had one thing in common- the students really cared. And because of that they came to be known by the sick, who appreciated them most, as angels of mercy.

On surgical 'ward ten' Tuesday morning was particularly busy. Patients were going to, and returning from operating theatres. Consultants, surgeons and interns were busy doing their rounds.

As Molly went between the beds, checking observations, she did not notice the last female patient being wheeled into the ward.

But eventually she wandered over to that bed too.

'Hello there,' she said whispered, 'I'm just going to take your blood pressure.'

The woman tried to smile but her mouth and lips were swollen and dry from the anaesthetic. After wrapping the cloth of the sphygmometer around the woman's arm, Molly suddenly became aware that the lady was staring at the name badge pinned to her uniform. Molly smiled shyly and continued squeezing the instrument. Then, putting the stethoscope into her ears, she watched the mercury rise in the glass as she listened intently for the sound of a beat. Glancing at her patient, she suddenly became aware that the woman was staring at her. Then she saw an excitement flicker across her face.

'I see your name is Furlong, Nurse,' she whispered,' tell me what does the M stand for?'

'It's Molly, Molly Furlong.'

The woman let out a little gasp and then asked again more excitedly this time.

'You're Irish aren't ya, I can tell. Where do ya come from.'

'County Wexford, do you know it?'

The woman thought for a moment, then ignoring Molly's question quickly asked another one.

'Tell me Nurse who are your parents.'

'My father's is David Furlong and my mother well, she died when I was born, her name was Molly too, Molly Malone.'

'Oh my God,' the woman said as she broke out in a small cough.

'Are you alright?' said Molly, touching her hand gently.

The lady leaned forward in great pain as she tried to hold her chest while coughing. Swallowing hard, she continued,

'I'm okay, its just painful to cough. Tell me Nurse did ya know McDermotts Fish Shop in the Coombe in Dublin?'

'Oh yes,' replied Molly, 'that's an electrical shop now Daddy owns it. My Aunt Jessie died and left it to him.'

'Mrs. McDermott died?...'she said sadly, then after thinking for a moment the woman asked:

'When did she die?'

'It must be ten years ago now, she had Alzheimer's.'

'And what about her husband old J.J. is he still alive?'

'Oh no, he died in a car accident years before that. It was terrible. Aunt Hattie says Aunt Jessie never got over it.'

'The poor man.'

'Why, did you know them?' asked Molly, as she grew more excited at the thoughts of finding somebody in Liverpool who knew her family.

The woman put her hand up to her face in disbelief.

'I knew them and your Aunt Hattie's family too.' Then, reaching over to Molly, she squeezed her hand as she said emotionally:

'But Nurse… your Mother, you're not going to believe this, she was my best friend,' and a tear rolled down her cheek and fell on the pillow.

Molly put her equipment down on the locker and sat on the edge of the bed.

'Why, what's your name?' she asked curiously.

'Roseanne, I'm Roseanne White,' she said quietly.

Molly thought for a moment. That name sounded familiar, where had she heard it before? Then she remembered

'Oh Fr. William told me something. Did you used to hang around together when you were all young.'

Roseanne smiled as she remembered William. She could still see him as a small boy in short trousers heading to school.

'How is he? Sur' he's must be a bishop by now.'

'Not at all he's quite happy as a curate and he's one of the best.'

'Oh I know,' said Roseanne, with a faraway look, 'he was awful kind to me.'

Suddenly the Sister-in-charge came marching down the ward. Looking crossly over at her student nurse, she said coldly:

'You know you're not allowed sit on the beds Nurse, and when you're finished there will you come to my office please, I need to go over some charts.'

'Yes sister,' said Molly as obediently she jumped to her feet.

Then as the sister passed on to the next bed, she bent down and whispered to Roseanne that soon as she was off duty she would return that evening for a chat.

Watching her best friend's daughter walk away Roseanne could not take her eyes off her. Suddenly old memories came flooding back. Once more she was with Molly Malone shopping on Grafton Street and going to the pictures.

Suddenly Roseanne winced in pain as she tried to settle herself on the pillows. The intravenous drip in situ in her left hand restricted her movements. Clutching her flat chest she still missed the familiar soft curves where her breasts used to be. As more tears ran down her face she looked over at the nurses office.

Then, catching sight of Molly Malone's daughter talking with the Sister, a strange calmness came over her, and a smile came to her lips. For the first time in many years she felt she was not alone.

Chapter 10.

It was after visiting hours when Molly came back to Ward Ten to talk with Roseanne. The other patients had settled down for the night, and she hoped that they would all have a good rest. With the curtains drawn around her bed, Roseanne lay in the dim light, propped up with many pillows.

'How are you feeling now? 'asked Molly, touching her forehead caringly.

'The tablets are keepin' the pain at bay but I'm very sore.'

The scent of her expensive perfume wafted in the air, and, together with her beautiful nightdresses, brought a touch of luxury to what was otherwise a very clinical ward. Hoping to lift her spirits Molly commented on the loveliness of them both. Immediately Roseanne insisted that Molly take a generous spray of the perfume.

'Are you sure?' asked Molly as she picked up the pretty bottle.

'Oh yeah, it reminds me of the times your mother and I tested every perfume bottle in Woolworths, and then went home smelling like I don't know what.' she said laughing.

Molly sprayed the exotic fragrance on her neck and both wrists. Then she sat back to listen to the escapades the four friends got up to in the old days. Having recalled the time Molly's mother fell and cut her hand, Roseanne said seriously:

'It was yer mother ya know that asked Seamus Thornton to become a doctor, and ya know somethin? she'd be very proud that yer a nurse today.'

Molly was delighted to hear that. Then Roseanne's face took on a very sad expression.

'I couldn't believe it when David wrote and told me she was dead. Oh! Molly she was so full of life. She loved your daddy so much. It was so sad. I went home for the funeral and everybody was broken-hearted. William cried at the grave and couldn't continue the prayers.'

'Aunt Hattie never told me that.'

'Oh indeed he did, sure everyone was cryin'.'

Staring blankly at the ceiling, she continued:

'I haven't been home since, I lost touch with them all.'

As they talked, the drug in the syringe caused Roseanne to drift off to sleep and Molly sat waiting patiently for her to wake up again. On one occasion Roseanne reached for Molly's hand. With a great urgency said:

'Would you do me a favour Molly?'

'Yes of course, what is it?'

'Would you write and ask William if he could come and visit me, I'd love to see him before…I mean I'd love to see him again.'

Molly reassured her that she would write that very evening.

Two days later Fr. William opened an important letter from Liverpool. He was amazed to learn how Roseanne had turned up on the very ward that Molly was working on. But reading on, a dreadful sense of sorrow came over him when he realized his childhood friend was dying. By the time he had finished the letter he had a great urge to go to Roseanne.

Having managed to obtain special leave of absence William flew into Speke Airport two days later. Molly was there to meet him, and in the taxi on the way back to the hospital, she filled him in on Roseanne's condition.

'She had a mastectomy eighteen months ago, followed by a course of chemotherapy, but unfortunately she's developed secondary's. She's had those removed now, but I'm afraid it does not look good, she could slip away anytime,' she said sadly.

'And she's still quite young,' said William thoughtfully.

Arriving at the hospital, they went immediately to Ward Ten.

The curtains were drawn around her bed, but for a fleeting moment, through a split in the drapes, William caught a glimpse of Roseanne. Sitting up in the bed supported by two nurses, her head lay sideways on her shoulders. Her blonde wig was a complete contrast to the black hair of her childhood. Her thin drawn face and dark eyes were not of the happy go lucky girl he once knew, but rather of someone in great suffering. Not recognising her, he turned to Molly and whispered anxiously:

'Are you sure that's her?' he asked worriedly.

'Oh yes that's Roseanne alright,' she whispered, the nurses will be finished attending to her in a minute and then we can go in.'

When Fr. William stepped up to the bed he made a great effort to smile and sound cheerful. For a few moments Roseanne stared at him in disbelief. Suddenly her eyes flickered with a youthful excitement.

Recognizing now the familiar girl he once knew, a great surge of emotion came over him. Sitting down on the bed he took her hand in both of his, leaned over and kissed her on the forehead.

'Thanks for comin'' she whispered.

'Rosie, dear Rosie of course I'd come.' he said tears filling his eyes.

As Molly looked on, she swallowed hard. Witnessing the happiness they were both experiencing caused tears to well up in her eyes. Then, deciding that she was not needed, she tiptoed out of the ward and left the two old friends alone.

Still holding Roseanne's hand, William pulled up a chair and sat down beside the bed.

'I'm afraid this time it has me,' she said as tears welled up in her eyes, 'and I'm so tired of fightin' it you know, so very tired. When they first told me I had cancer the shock was like the anaesthetic. It numbed my feelin's against what I had to face.'

William bowed his head and continued to stroke her hand. A tremendous sense of helplessness came over him.

'You were always a brave girl in the past,' he said encouragingly, 'don't give up now.'

'Oh I think that girl you remember is long gone,' she said wiping her tears awkwardly with the back of her hand.

'No she's not.'

'But you know William, what's worse is people's ignorance and fear about cancer. It isolates ya know in a way that makes ya feel like a leper.'

'Rosie, don't talk like that... you know Molly and I are here to help.'

'Isn't she beautiful, 'wouldn't our Moll have been so proud of her?'

Getting quite emotional for a moment, William nodded in total agreement.

'You know, it doesn't seem that long ago,' said Roseanne wistfully

'I suppose it doesn't,' said Fr. William. Then wanting to change the subject he asked;

'Tell me what happened to you after, Rosie? Where did you go? Tell me everything,' he said, sitting back in the chair.

For the first time that evening Roseanne smiled and in her old cheeky way said:

'Now William I can't be tellin' you everything, you bein' a priest and all, but I'll tell ya what I'll do, I'll tell ya the best bits.'

William could not help chuckling at her familiar witty reply.

Taking a deep breath she began to tell him what life had been like since Molly and he had left her to the boat all those years ago. How she had stayed in the home and given birth to a son. Then, having reluctantly given the child up for adoption, she managed to get a job in a pub in Manchester.

'The landlord- Ronnie- he has been very good to me, and over the years, well, him and me, we have a sort of an understandin'.'

'Did you ever marry?' asked William.

'No I didn't, mind ya Ronnie wanted me to, God knows he asked me often enough, but ya see I didn't have the courage.'

The two friends sat and talked most of the afternoon. With the nurses interrupting every so often to attend to Roseanne needs, and Roseanne herself drifting in and out of sleep, William feared that he might tire her out.

'I'll go and let you rest,' he whispered on one occasion.

'No... no,' she protested, 'I'm fine, I want to talk to you. Would you be able to stay on here for a bit?'

'Well I've managed to get some time off, I can't promise Rosie, but I'll stay as long as I can.'

Giving a great sigh of relief, she lay back on the pillows.

'You're close to Nurse Molly aren't ya?' she asked curiously.

'But sur, my mother reared her.'

'How come?'

'Well, after her mother died David got it very hard to settle. Then J.J. died and Jessie McDermott was so upset she became very ill. Mother looked after Molly from the day she was born, and not wanting to move the child around, David thought it best if the child stayed with her permanently.'

Roseanne began thinking back. 'Aye after any heartbreak peace is hard to find.'

'Tell me, have you found peace Rosy?'

With a rather sad, faraway look in her eyes she replied,

'No I never did... and that's one of the reasons I sent for you.'

Pointing to the locker beside her bed she asked William to take out a large brown envelope from it. When he had done so she reached out and clutched his hand tightly,

'Will you find him for me William?'

'Find who Roseanne?'

With a deep sigh she said quietly, 'My son.'

Taken aback, William protested, 'But Roseanne that might be difficult. These things can take a long time.'

'Please William, I already know where he lives, but I could never bring meself to meet him. Will you help me to do this, I haven't got much time.'

Seeing how anxious she had become, William eased her back on the pillows.

'Okay, I'll do what I can. But first I'm going to see about booking into a hotel. Now you get some rest and I'll come back tomorrow.'

As he turned to leave, he made the sign of the cross on her forehead.

'God bless you,' he said, bending over and kissing her again.

Roseanne could not reply for tears of sheer relief were rolling down her cheeks.

As William walked out of the ward, he purposely concentrated on happy memories to help fight back his own tears, now threatening to fall. Then, as he looked down at the envelope his expression changed. Only now was he beginning to think that maybe it would be better to leave the past alone.

Chapter 11.

Seamus Thornton stood by the fireplace watching his children and their little friends blow out the candles on a large chocolate cake. Then they all gathered around the excited baby to sing Happy Birthday. But Seamus, being unmoved by their laughter, walked over to the drinks cabinet and poured himself out a whisky

Then, sitting down in the armchair, he watched with amusement as the children helped to open the many colourful boxes they had brought as presents.

Looking over at his wife Eithne, he could not help thinking how happy and contented she looked in the midst of all the other women. She seemed totally absorbed in her job as she began pouring out soft drinks and handing around the party food. Now and again one of the children would run over excitedly to show Seamus their toys and distract him from his serious thoughts.

He loved his children dearly and thanked God that they were all healthy.

But in the midst of this family gathering Seamus was feeling very lonely. Deep down he knew that in the one short year since his wife had their last baby, their relationship had deteriorated.

So swallowing down the last of his drink, he made excuses that he was wanted at the hospital, stood up and left the room.

Getting in his car, he turned on the radio and decided to go for a long drive. He needed time to himself to think. He decided to take the coast road and drive out towards Howth. The sight of the sea stretching before him gave him a great feeling of escape. Feeling as he did, all a man could do was escape, go anywhere, to pubs, clubs, golf courses anywhere, just to get away.

Suddenly he caught sight of two young lovers sitting on a park bench. Engrossed in their kisses, they were totally oblivious of the stares of passers-by.

As Seamus watched them his mind flashed back to when Eithne and he were courting. For a fleeting moment he felt everything they were feeling. He remembered the excitement and the passion. But then driving in traffic, he quickly lost sight of them and his mind returned to its lonely state.

Suddenly angry feelings began to rise inside him. It was now a year since the birth of their last child. Eithne was still stubbornly refusing to take any form of contraceptive. Their lovemaking had become most frustrating as Seamus tried hard to avoid another child. Most of the time their efforts ended in rows, and lately they had started to avoid it altogether. Seamus had begun to work late at the hospital and sometimes he slept over. Driving along now, he could hear his friend Gary's words of advice in his head.

'They're all the same you know, women, as soon as they get the ring on their finger and the baby under their arm they don't want you. Oh I know all about it. Now Seamus what you want is a bit on the side. Everybody does it. Nobody need know and nobody gets hurt.'

Thinking about it now those words were beginning to ring true. But deep down he had one small problem, Seamus still loved his wife. Banging his fist on the steering wheel, he said out loud:

'God damn it I should be able to make love to her without her getting pregnant all the time.'

He began thinking back to the days before the children came, to the excitement, the teasing, the thrills and the passion. From the moment he met her he had found her to be a very vibrant exciting woman. They would steal away together from the crowd just to be with each other. Then, once alone, one touch was enough to light a burning fire of desire between them.

Suddenly those memories were taken over by awful feelings of rejection. Slowly they had been building up inside him over the last few years.

'What the hell am I going to do,' he thought,' I can't go on like this. I'm a man, I need to make love to my wife.'

Then a wild fantasy took over.

He began imaging he went back to his house, walked in on the party, took her by the hand and together they drove away.

Then with the hot sun on their backs they walked hand in hand between the sand dunes. He stood behind her kissing the back of her long sexy neck. She moved her head slowly from side to side with sheer pleasure. Then he unzipped her light summer dress down to the base of her spine.

His eager hands moved sensuously and slowly around her body and up to her breasts. Holding their fullness, he pressed his body closer as she intertwined her arms around his neck. Then, together, they sank down onto the warm sand.

As Seamus's blood rose to the excitement of his imagination, a car suddenly blew its horn loudly from behind. Failing to see the red light change to green, he waved apologetically to the driver, and quickly drove on. With his fantasy now gone, he felt worse than before.

'Fat chance of that ever happening,' he thought sadly.

A little while later he arrived at Howth harbour. After parking his car he got out and walked towards the pier. Strolling along, the sun warmed his back as the sea breeze cooled his face. Noisy, swift seagulls dipped and dived as they flew overhead. Walking to the end of the pier, he sat for a long time watching the fishing and sailing boats coming and going. At one stage he wished he could just hop on a vessel and get away from it all.

But he did not, and after a while, feeling a little chilled, he turned back and walked to the Saint Lawrence Hotel for some hot coffee.

That night Dr. Thonrton could be found, as usual, in Holles Street Hospital doing his rounds. At break time he headed down the corridor towards the canteen. After pressing a button, the sliding doors of the lift opened and he stepped inside.

Standing in a corner of the lift, a pretty young nurse smiled at him. With his frustration and loneliness making him quite vulnerable her friendly smile went straight to his heart. In it he read a thousand messages.

Then, with a boyish twinkle in his eyes, Seamus turned and, in an instant, found himself smiling right back.

Chapter 12.

Yes indeed, all the information concerning Roseanne's son, Fr. William found was in the large brown envelope she gave him. Especially one letter in particular. It was from the Archer family. In it they stated, that from the beginning they had told the boy he was adopted. They had given him the name Edgar, and went on to say they had no objection if his natural mother wanted to make contact with him.

As William took the train journey up to Leeds, despite his misgivings, he wanted desperately to bring Roseanne some peace.

Now travelling back to Liverpool with Edgar, William broke the awkward silence and began to explain what it was like for any pregnant unmarried woman in Ireland all those years ago. Desperately not wanting him to judge his mother or feel any resentment towards her, William tried to point out to Edgar the advantages he had been given by being adopted.

Then listening in turn to the well spoken young man, William could not help but be impressed. At the age of twenty-four Edgar had a great lifestyle. With his insurance business expanding by the day, he knew exactly where he was going and what he wanted out of life.

'Does she have any other family over here?' he asked William.

'No, just Ronnie Wilcox, a publican she worked with. Apparently he has been very good to her. I have not met him yet as he comes to visit her late in the mornings. The pub is a very busy one I've been told.'

For the rest of the journey Fr. William was spared any more questions and relaxed a little. He found himself enjoying the smooth fast drive to Liverpool in Edgar's brand new Jaguar.

By the time they had arrived at the hospital he had sadly told the young man what to expect.

As they approached her bed Roseanne lay sleeping. William sat down in the chair and stroked the back of her hand gently.

Opening her heavy eyelids ever so slowly, Roseanne looked up at the unfamiliar figure standing awkwardly at the end of her bed.

Slowly turning her head, she looked at William in a puzzled manner.

'Yes Rosie,' he said smiling,' this is your son Edgar.'

'Oh help me sit up.' she said excitedly.

William fluffed up the pillows at her back, then he beckoned to Edgar to come closer and sit in his chair.

Pulling clumsily at the bedclothes, Roseanne embarrassingly tried to cover her deformed chest.

Then taking a closer look at her visitor she saw a well dressed stocky young man standing beside her. In contrast to her pale, weak, wasting body, his young strong tanned one exuded health. Desperately she searched his tanned face. The young man smiled and in an instant, revealed that attractive smirk that had captured her heart all those years ago. Holding back from calling out Tommo's name, Roseanne looked in amazement at him.

William squeezed her feet reassuringly as he moved to the other side of her bed. Then, taking another chair, he sat next to the locker.

Looking back up at her son, Roseanne's lips began to tremble as her eyes filled up with tears.

'I'm glad ya came,' she whispered, reaching her thin hand out to him. Edgar, seemingly unmoved, took her hand and smiled graciously.

Then Roseanne let out a deep sigh.

'I've wanted to see ya for such a long time,' she said, 'I wanted to tell ya, only now I don't know where to begin.'

With her breathing quick and shallow, she moved uncomfortably on the pillows.

'Its alright, don't distress yourself,' said Edgar, still unconcerned.

'But ya have to know,' she went on,' I need ya to know what happened. It all started out so wonderful, I really loved your Da, and you know somethin? you look just like him, except for your hair,' then in a choked voice she said affectionately, 'I think that's mine.'

'You see Edgar,' she went on,'...I really thought that he loved me. But then... anyway, when I found out I was expecting, things changed. In those days it was a dreadful disgrace and me family put me out. I was only nineteen, younger than you are now, and I didn't know what to do.'

With her mouth feeling very dry, Roseanne tried to lick her lips.

Fr. William reached for the glass of water and held her head as she took a small sip.

'Oh Edgar, I never wanted to give ya up,' she said lying back breathless on the pillows. 'But what else could I do? Ya would have had no life with me, no real chance.'

'I understand,' said Edgar, still unmoved, as he watched Roseanne drift into a drugged sleep.

The two men sat silently facing one another as they waited for her to wake up again. William took a tissue from the locker and gently wiped both corners of her mouth. In a matter of minutes her eyes opened again.

'I'm sorry son,' she whispered, 'I'm so sorry. I wish I had the strength… never a day went by but I thought about ya. Can you ever forgive me?'

Edgar looked blankly at Fr.William and then back to Roseanne.

'There's nothing to forgive,' he said casually, 'I have a good life, there's no need for you to have any regrets.'

'So you're really happy then?' asked Roseanne hopefully.

'Yes I am actually.'

'Oh I'm so glad,' she said, letting out a great sigh of relief.

Then, turning to William, she pointed to the locker,' There's a little red box in there would ya take it out for me please.'

William handed it to her and, looking down at it thoughtfully, she began stroking it with her thumbs. Then taking Edgar's hand, she placed the box firmly in his palm.

'It's a ring your Da gave me many years ago. It's very important to me that you have it.'

Edgar opened the box and smiled as he looked at the ring.

'I want you to know,' Roseanne whispered, 'that despite what happened after, that ring is the symbol of the love your Da and I shared when you were conceived.'

Edgar thanked her and patted her hand.

Just then Molly came in with another nurse to attend to her needs. William stood up and introduced Roseanne's son to them both.

The attractive smile once more spread across Edgar's face as he raised Molly's hand to his lips and kissed it. Molly blushed deeply and looked over at her giggling work mate.

'I'm afraid you'll have to excuse us and wait outside for a bit,'she said, covering her embarrassment.

'We'll call back tonight,' said William, but Roseanne did not hear as she had already drifted off into another sleep.

As the two men left the hospital William thanked Edgar for his understanding and told him how much it meant to his mother.

'Will you be able to stay on for a while?' he asked hopefully. William was surprised when he readily agreed to do so.

But when they returned that evening to the hospital Roseanne had slipped into a coma. The two men went in and sat each side of the bed. William invited Edgar to pray with him.

'If you don't mind I'd rather not, I don't believe any of that stuff,' he said sharply.

Slightly taken aback, William said nothing. Then he looked down at Roseanne and started a prayer. The awkward silence was broken when Molly stuck her head around the curtains.

'I'm going off duty now,' she whispered, 'but I'll call back later.'

Excusing himself Edgar followed her down the corridor. Catching up with her at the lift he said cheerfully, 'Excuse me Molly, but would you mind awfully if I asked you to join me. We could get something to eat and maybe you could tell more about my mother.'

Molly smiled up at him as a tingle of excitement ran through her.

In the long dark night that followed Roseanne battled for every breath.

With the heaviness of death hanging over her William prepared to give her the last rites. Then he sat, sometimes praying, sometimes reading but always holding her hand.

Next morning as the nurses changed shifts, he was the only one with her when her heart went from a strong steady beat, to a little flutter, and finally stopped altogether. Tears streamed down his face as he watched her slip silently and peacefully away. Leaning over her now restful body, he stroked her hair tenderly.

'Goodbye Roseanne,' he whispered, 'I hope we meet again.'

In the office Molly asked Sister Woods to be excused from the task of laying the body out. She could not coldly write her name on her leg, or tie a label around her toes, for this time it was too personal.

The following evening as Roseanne's remains were driven away in a long black hearse, a little girl strolled past the hospital on her way to school. Suddenly she noticed a small red box lying in a tuft of grass. Reaching in through the iron railing, she pushed and struggled with all her might to pick it up. Eventually she got it, and pulling her small sore arm back out she pulled down her sleeve and opened the box curiously. Then she let out an excited gasp when she saw a beautiful shiny ring. Shutting the box quickly, she looked cautiously around to see if the owner might be looking. But on seeing the coast was clear, she quickly hid it in her pocket and ran happily down the street.

CHAPTER 13.

'You know, you have it all,' said Deirdre as she looked around the kitchen.

'What do you mean?' asked Eithne as she continued feeding the baby its lunch.

'Well you have this beautiful house, five adorable children, a gorgeous husband, plenty of money. I tell you I'd swap places with you anytime.'

'Well,' said Eithne, smiling happily at her friend, 'I suppose I do have a lot to be thankful for.'

'Mind you,' said Deirdre, reaching for another cigarette. 'Seamus can't be working late all the time, sur there must be some other reason he doesn't come home. Aren't you worried at all?'

Eithne was aware of what her friend was hinting at. But she was not going to give her the satisfaction of seeing that she had upset her.

'I trust my husband,' she said in a confident voice,' and I've more to do with my time than worry about him.'

However, later when her friend had gone home, Eithne found herself going over her hurtful remarks. Little doubts and worries began to creep into her mind. But having thought about them, she decided not to go there and stay instead with her first way of thinking.

She had always said from the beginning of their marriage that she would not be a possessive wife. She wanted their relationship to be based on trust instead of demanding possessiveness. In committing themselves to each other, she felt that they both had the right to be free to express their individuality.

She knew her husband loved her and because of that she was confident that he would never do anything that would hurt her. Her friend could hint all she liked but Eithne had one advantage, she was Seamus's wife and the mother of his children.

Later, looking in her bedroom mirror, she ran her hands over her hips. She had put on more than a little weight over the last few years. Taking the measuring tape from the drawer, she was upset to see her twenty four inch waist now measured thirty. There and then she decided she would go on a diet. It was Seamus and William's 45th birthday in a couple of months and Eithne had toyed with the idea of throwing a surprise party for them both. Now, having made her mind up, she was determined that over the next few weeks she was going to look great for the occasion.

With the older children in school and only the baby at home, she also decided to make some changes. The young girl, Rose, who came in twice a week to help with the housework was only too pleased to do some extra days.

Cutting down on her food, Eithne began to take more time to exercise and relax. A week before the party she took the whole day off and headed into town. She searched all the shops for the perfect dress to show off her new slim figure. Finally in Switzers department store the assistant showed her one in particular. It was a slim fitting sleeveless cocktail dress of deep blue satin, and she knew immediately that it was exactly what she wanted. Slipping it over her head, the assistant helped with the zipper.

As Eithne caught sight of her reflection in the mirror, for the first time in almost eight years she felt like a desirable woman. All the fat, clumsy memories of pregnancy had disappeared and in their place stood a slim confident woman beaming with happiness. The more she looked at her reflection the more certain she became that this dress would definitely help to get her husband to fall in love with her all over again.

A few nights later the street outside no. 28 was lined on both sides with cars. Couples and old friends walked up the short steps to be met by a radiant looking Eithne. Standing in the hall, she shook hands and instantly made everyone feel very welcome.

Then looking over one of the guest's shoulders she saw Julie arrive. Excusing herself, she rushed out to meet her. Taking two colourful packages from her arms she helped the old lady up the steps.

'I'm glad you made it,' she whispered affectionately. The housekeeper patted her hand reassuringly:

'Sur. I wouldn't miss it for the world, has herself arrived yet?' she asked curiously.

'No. I'm afraid the doctor wouldn't let Hattie come, she still has a touch of flu. But she sends her love and wants you to visit her and tell her all about tonight.'

'Well I'll certainly do that,' said Julie. patting her hand.

Gary, one of Seamus's colleagues. had brought the two brothers out earlier for a drink. Eithne now looked excitedly up and down the street as she waited for their return.

A half an hour later, and on a false pretence, Gary persuaded the birthday boys to return to the house. Ethine and Julie huddled quietly with the rest of the guests in the darkness of the sitting room. Between comments and jokes they tried very hard not to make a sound. When Seamus flicked the light switch and walked into the room everyone stood up and shouted 'Surprise Surprise.'

From the corner of the room Eithne stood back from the crowd. A great surge of love swept over her as she watched the delighted expression on her husband's face. All the effort she had put into this special night had been worth it. Wanting to be close to him she walked across the room.

'When did you plan all this?' he whispered as he shook their guests hands.

'A while ago,' she said, smiling up at him.

'Well it's certainly a great surprise,' he said as he moved away to greet somebody else.

Eithne was a little hurt that he did not show the expected reaction to her appearance. Once again she found herself making excuses for him. Then swallowing her disappointment, she turned to mingle with their friends.

From the corner of his eye Seamus watched her closely. He had wanted so much to tell her how beautiful she was but when she looked at him with such love and openness in her eyes, guilty feelings about his flirtations suddenly came between them.

Now as he watched her, he could not recall when he had ever seen her look so lovely. In her clinging dress her figure looked amazing. The shimmer of the fabric set off the new blonde colour in her hair, and her high shoes gave her legs a very sexy shape. As she moved among their friends his guilt made him feel unworthy of her and so he decided to keep away.

The party went on in full swing into the early hours of the morning. Everyone enjoyed the delicious food as the buffet went down a treat.

Fr. William was delighted to meet and chat to old friends he had not seen since school days. For once Julie was the guest and given the most comfortable armchair as a mark of honour. Relaxing and enjoying herself, she began, after a few drinks, to tell stories of the mischievous antics the twins had got up to in their young days. Everyone listened with great interest and the whole room erupted with laughter from time to time. But as she reminisced she suddenly got up from the chair, walked over, and put her arms around them both. With tears welling up in her eyes she looked up affectionately at Seamus and Fr.William.

'Ah but yer still our boys,' she said fondly.

The two men bent down and hugged her tightly.

By 2 a.m the party began to wind down and some of the guests had left to go home. Seamus reached for some water to pour into his drink. Seeing the jug empty, he got up and went out towards the kitchen. The door was slightly ajar and as he approached it, he could hear two familiar voices deep in conversation.

Peeping in he saw Eithne and his friend Gary standing at the sink washing up.

'You know, Seamus is a lucky man. I was admiring you earlier on and I'd never believe you had all those babies, you look terrific.' Gary said as he took a plate from her.

Ethine blushed as she whispered, 'Thank you.'

'That's a very sexy dress,' he continued.

Eithne turned and beamed a flirting smile up at him.

This was exactly what she had wanted to hear but unfortunately the wrong man was saying it.

Seamus stood at the door watching them laughing and joking. At one stage Gary slapped Eithine playfully on the behind with the tea towel. Suddenly for the first time ever jealous feelings rose up inside Seamus.

Returning to the sitting room, he swallowed his neat whisky in one gulp.

It was only now, having witnessed another man getting too close to his wife, that he realized what he might lose.

Chapter 14.

Eithne Thornton began undressing. From the comfort of their brass bed her husband watched her every move. His excitement was like a fire burning in his eyes. Having gracefully slipped out of her beautiful red dress she walked over and hung it in the wardrobe. Then she went to remove her pretty lace underwear.

'No leave those on,' he said as he reached his hand out to her.

Feeling thrilled by his comment she turned, flashed him a special smile and slipped eagerly into the bed beside him.

Oh how good his strong warm hands felt as they slid effortlessly over the smooth silk of her new undergarments. With her passion being already stirred by the buzz off the party, and the consumption of a little alcohol, Eithne relaxed and enjoyed her husband's attentions.

Then, when he reached for the back of her neck, and held it firmly, they both began to kiss more intensely.

'How do I get you out of these things?' he said with an urgent whisper. As he chewed playfully on her ear Eithne suddenly remembered what time of the month it was. With the fear of pregnancy now foremost in her mind she said regretfully,

'I'm sorry Seamus but if we do it tonight I'll get pregnant.'

With those words she could instantly feel his body go rigid. Kissing her lightly on the cheek he just turned over and lay with his back to her. Once more that dreadful silence descended on the bedroom.

Eithne, not wanting the cuddling and kisses to stop, snuggled tightly into his back and put her arm around him

At the feel of her touch Seamus leaped, as if scalded by a pot of hot water, and jumped out of the bed. Once more familiar feelings of rejection caused an anger to rise up inside him.

'I thought you wanted me,' he said angrily,' Obviously I was mistaken.'

'No that's not true I do want you,' she protested.

'God, with the way you were dressed tonight, even down to that gorgeous underwear... I was sure you wanted me. You know after seeing you flirting in the kitchen with Gary, I'm beginning to think you're just one big tease.'

With that, he took the cover off the bed stormed from the room and went down the stairs.

Eithne lay back on the pillows. Her husband was not only very angry with her but had accused her of doing something that she would never do.

Now, looking down at her underwear, they suddenly seemed cheap and sluttish. Getting up from the bed she removed and threw them angrily across the room. Then, putting her dressing gown on, she pulled it tightly around her, sat down on the bed, and started to cry. Meanwhile down in the sitting room Seamus lay on the settee. The alcohol he had consumed at the party was now taking effect and he felt very sleepy. Wanting to shut the world out, he wrapped the cover around him and drifted off into an unhappy sleep. Sitting upstairs in the darkness Ethel sat thinking.

Since her first baby was born ten years ago she was fed up dodging, taking chances, and sometimes getting pregnant. She was fed up with the numerous rows, and worse still, the insufferable silences. So she decided she would do something about it. For the past year she had carefully charted and noted her fertility. It had taken a long time, but at last, without any tablets or contraptions she had taken control of her own body. This gave her a great feeling of well being and satisfaction.

But now all the effort she had put in over the last few months seemed to be for nothing.

So, feeling now that she too could not take much more, she stood up and hurried downstairs.

Opening the door of the sitting room she switched on the bright overhead light. Seamus screwed up his sleepy eyes in an effort to see.

'I want to talk to you Seamus,' she said as she stood over him.

'I'm tired, go back to bed.'

'No I won't go back to bed, its nearly morning anyway and I have to talk to you.'

Looking at his watch Seamus said anxiously:

'I'm on duty in five hours, I have to get some sleep.'

Then rather childishly he turned over and pulled the quilt up over his head.

Eithne reached over and pulled it back down.

'I don't care if you never work again, we're going to talk about this once and for all.'

'There's nothing to talk about,' he said sarcastically

'You don't want sex, I'm fed up trying so we'll leave it. But I'm telling you now there is plenty of women out there who do.'

'That's unfair,' said Ethine as his remark hurt her deeply.

'Well what else am I supposed to think.'

Then, noticing her tearstained unhappy face, he sat up and said wearily: 'Alright then go on, I'm listening.'

Eithne sat down at the end of the couch, took a deep breath and began:

'Seamus when I was young I used to play games with my brothers. I was strong and wild and sometimes I'd win. At that time I didn't feel there was any difference between us. Then I became a teenager and I became aware of changes taking place in my body. Suddenly I didn't want to play their games anymore. I found them too rough.

Then when I was fifteen I started to go to dances. My parents told me I was a young lady now and that I should respect myself. I had no reason to doubt their advice because everything they said gave me a sense of dignity and made me feel good. I always wanted to save myself for that special man who would come along. Then I met you and we fell in love straight away."

They both smiled awkwardly at each other as they remembered that first meeting.

'When we were courting I remember how free I felt in expressing my love for you. Do you remember the passionate times we had in the forest and down by the lake?'

'Yes I do,' said Seamus,' but you've changed since then, you've become more of a mother figure.'

Ignoring his silly remark Ethel continued:

'Do you know why I felt so free? Because you respected me then and I knew I wouldn't get pregnant.'

'Well if I remember we both decided we would wait until we got married.'

'Yes but then everything changed. You wanted it almost every night and whenever I told you no, you took it that I didn't want you.'

Sitting up Seamus grew angry again. 'But you don't seem to realize that that's what married people do, they make love. Now if you'd only stop being stubborn and take some form of contraception we wouldn't be having this argument.'

Suddenly Eithne realised that she would not only have to defend her right not to take contraception, but she would have to defend her complex womanhood as well."

'God Seamus, you as a doctor should know there can be harmful side effects to some of those contraceptives. Do you not think I have thought long and hard about all this? Every time I gave birth I knew I could have died. And if I had, I would have died alone because you were never there.'

Ashamedly, Seamus's gaze fell to the floor.

'Look at me, I'm your wife. I'm not something to be taken whenever the humour takes you. I'm not a baby-making machine that knows no end, I'm a woman. By taking contraception, I'd feel my sensitive hormones would be controlled by a drug. Don't you see, the natural passions and moods I experience through these hormones, are driven also by the grace in my soul, the love in my heart and the thoughts in my mind. This pill would, as well as the harmful physical side effects, make me sexually available to you at all times, and I would become like a man. I fear for the loss of my femininity which is related to my dignity.'

'Now you're being silly you know that wouldn't happen.'

'Oh yes it would. How many times before have you blamed me for getting pregnant? It was like I made the mistake and conceived the child. It was like I had to live with the consequence instead of enjoying the child.'

Then, with tears welling up in her eyes, she said with a quivering lip:

'There were times when, God forgive me, I was under such pressure to please you sexually that I even contemplated getting rid of our child.'

Reaching over, he took her hand in his. 'Now that's not true, I never put pressure on you. Tell me what did I ever say?'

'You didn't say it with words you said it with your silence.'

Not really understanding her he continued:

'But other women don't seem to have your problem with contraception.'

After thinking for a few moments she pulled her hand away, stood up and shouted,

'Seamus stop talking about other women, I am me.'

Then pointing to herself with both hands she said angrily:

'I have to live in this body. I want to experience its impulsive changes and its fiery moods. There are times when I need lovemaking and there are times when I don't. There are days when it is impossible and there are days when it's not. I want to go through the menopause and enter into a dignified old age knowing that I have always listened to, and respected the needs of my body. No matter how hard it may be I want to discover it all. I didn't design this body so I can't take the blame for it. But one thing I do know, I want to live in it in its natural state. I don't want chemicals or gadgets to surpress any part of it. If it has to be controlled then I want my mind to be strong enough to do it. So until you can understand me, you'll never accept the complexity of my womanhood and I won't have the freedom to express all of my love.'

Seamus reached for her again.

'Don't be getting yourself all upset, you know I love you.'

Pulling back from him, her eyes flashed with more frustration as she replied:

'Do I you? Love is proved by deeds not words. How many times have you shut me out? Its like you want to feed on the pleasure that I can give you. It's like you want to take of me all the time. But I am not a bottomless pit of giving. Sometimes you are so preoccupied with your own desires that you become almost resentful of my differences. But those feminine differences should be equally respected and accepted as your male ones are.'

Then Seamus began to raise his voice too as he protested:

'But you don't know what it's like for a man, it's awful to feel rejected.'

A familiar silence descended on the room. Eithne was the first to break it.'

'So,' she said quietly,' what you're saying is, if I could have sexual intercourse with you all the time you wouldn't feel rejected… you'd feel loved is that what your saying?'

'Well yes I suppose so.'

Walking towards the door, she suddenly turned and looked back very disappointedly at her husband.

'Well if that's all love is to you, I feel very sorry for you,' and with that she stormed out of the room and banged the door.

Awake now, Seamus got up and walked around the room.

Her words were burning in his brain. He went over them again and again. Suddenly he began to feel ashamed and slightly embarrassed at his behaviour in the past. It was tonight of all nights, on his 45th birthday, that the whole issue of lovemaking had come to a head.

Chapter 14.

Seamus Thornton, wanting to make things up with his wife, walked quietly up the stairs and into their bedroom. He had tried to go back to sleep earlier, but his wife's words had really stung him. So for the few hours that remained of what had been a very long night, he sat and thought very deeply about everything. Now feeling guilty, he realised that the time had come to apologize and tell her just how he felt.

Walking over to the bed, he sat down gently and watched her sleeping. Her lovely thick blonde hair lay tousled around her face. Instead of lying on her own side of the bed, her body was stretched out in all directions. The continental quilt looked like it had wrestled a lion to get some sleep.

Seamus smiled down tenderly at the only woman he had ever truly loved. He went to touch her but hesitated and drew back.

Instead he decided to just sit and watch her sleeping for a few more moments.

Lying in the morning light she looked more like a little girl than a grown woman, much less the mother of his five children. Bending down to her outstretched hand, he gently kissed her palm.

Opening her sleepy eyes, she looked up, almost baby like, into his face.

'I love you,' he whispered.

'What time is it?' she asked drowsily.

'It's half past eight,' he whispered tenderly

'That late, are the children awake yet?'

'No, don't worry, I looked in on them and they're out for the count. Even the baby, I think the party has them exhausted.'

Still speaking in a very low voice she inquired,

'Shouldn't you be at the hospital?'

'I rang in earlier and Gary's going to cover for me until this evening, although he says his head feels like a train ran through it.'

They both smiled at the thoughts of it.

Then reaching out, Seamus took her hand in his and said in a very sincere voice:

'Listen, I'm so sorry darling, I know I've been selfish, and it's not just that, but I feel I've been selfish in the male chauvinistic sense of the word. Remembering the intensity of their row Eithne looked up at him and said quietly:

'Its okay Seamus.'

'No,' he replied, getting up from the bed,' It's not okay. You see, looking back on it now, I was never really taught about sex. Both William and I, well we found out about it by listening to other boys. I suppose in a way you could say we grew up with a fear of sex. When we went to secondary school all the other boys used to talk about it as if it was great fun or some kind of conquest. Then later, I found medical school was no help either, as we were given a more clinical attitude to it.'

Then, walking back to the bed, he sat down beside her again.

'When I met you darling and we decided that we would wait until we were married I was somewhat relieved. Do you remember how awkward we both were the first night? I always felt I had disappointed you.'

'Oh no Seamus you were always such a flirt and so outgoing that I thought I had disappointed you.'

'But don't you see all that was just me covering up for my shyness. Then when you became pregnant, I can't really explain it, but I felt a manly power. It was a funny feeling really. It was only then that I started to discover the pleasures of making love to you. When we kissed, when I held you, I wanted more of you. But then the twins came and took up so much of your time. I was tied up with the hospital and when we did manage to snatch precious moments together, kisses and cuddles weren't enough. I wanted to recapture those first few months we had together. But even then I didn't have all of your attention, you always seemed to be listening for the children.'

'But it's so hard to forget that they're in the house.'

'Oh I'm not blaming you, but you were right about me not being at any of their births. There again I'm so sorry. But it was because of what happened to my friend Molly Malone that I couldn't face it. I was so afraid you might die too. Suddenly I realised what could go wrong and the risks you were taking. So I selfishly presumed that like any problem, I could stop it. Now that is where I made the mistake.'

Rubbing her arm tenderly, tears began to well up in his eyes.

'It's okay Seamus,' she said, putting her hand on his, 'I'm sorry I got angry last night but...'

'No, you made me realise something very important. I know now that if you started taking contraception it would take from that special magic you spoke about last night. So I've decided ...em...to get myself sterilized instead.'

Horrified at the thoughts of it, Eithne immediately got up from the bed and stood before him.

'No you're still not listening to me. I don't want either of us to interfere with our sexuality. Don't you know that you being able to give me children is one of the things that excites my passion?'

Scratching his head he looked at her in slight confusion,

'I never knew that.'

Well it's true, I have always felt that your masculinity was a powerful thing. I also love your rough skin, your coarse hair, your strong muscles and your deep voice. Whenever you hold me close the scent of your maleness excites me.'

'So what will we do then?'

With her eyes suddenly taking on a deep intensity, she looked straight into his and said challengingly:

'I want your love to be our contraception.'

An electrifying silence hung in the air as Seamus's eyes in turn reacted with an amazed expression.

Finding great relief at last from having expressed her true thoughts, Eithne now began to speak more quickly with a burning excitement in her voice.

'Oh Seamus there is no point in walking to the edge of a cliff if there is a rail around it. I need you to protect me. After all this time and having five babies together, I feel we haven't been totally honest with each other. I don't want our lovemaking to become a risk free easy habit. Instead I want you to really discover all of me and me the same with you. Not always in some heated burst of passion, which can be wonderful, but also in other ways. I want us to spend time finding out the deepest secrets of the rhythms and longings of our bodies which are unique to our own sex. From now on I'd like it be the giving and taking of also the spiritual part of our lovemaking, so that in sickness, worry or stress, one would wait patiently for the other.

I want to discover the depths and the heights in which our love could grow. Then maybe we could shut out all worldly advice, and find a sexual freedom that is unique to you and me. A freedom that will not be controlled, is not demanding but is so honest it will reach almost to the divine.'

Seamus stood rooted to the ground. This was the first time he had heard any of this. Her confidence in her words, expressed with such truth and passion, went straight to his heart. In the last few hours he had been so sure of his own argument, Now, after hearing all this, he suddenly became ashamed. 'If only other men could know this,' he thought to himself.

Then looking deep into her eyes, he said sincerely,

'But do you really think we could find all that?'

Eithne took him in her arms and in that moment her love for him swelled in her heart. For the first time in ever so long she felt a barrier lift between them. Looking down now at her rather childlike man she could not help but smile.

And with her eyes filling with tears she said almost gladly:

'Oh don't you see, there is nothing in this life only love, everything else is just a silly illusion.'

Chapter 15.

Kneeling down wearily on the bedroom floor, Fr. William found it hard to believe that it was five months since he had received that disturbing phone call from Molly in Liverpool. With his mind flashing over the events, he bowed his head in prayer.

Then, as he neared the end, he added one more. With deep gratitude, he thanked God for the privilege of being at the bedside of his childhood friend when she was dying. In all the sadness it comforted him to know that he had helped make Roseanne's death a peaceful one.

Closing his breviary, he got up from his knees and breathed a great sigh of relief. Then he pulled back the bedclothes and gratefully sank into the comfort of his own bed. Being totally exhausted as a result of battling with the flu a few weeks previously, he stretched out, and it was only a matter of minutes before he drifted into a deep sleep. Much later a constant tapping disturbed his well-earned rest

As his level of consciousness rose, he found the noise extremely annoying. Being half asleep, he found it hard to tell whether the tapping was in his dreams or reality.

After what seemed like ages he awoke and strained his ears to listen. The tapping stopped. Hoping he had imagined it, he was about to relax when the noise started up again. A little more awake now, he found it hard to make out what exactly the sound was. It seemed to be coming from downstairs and sounded like a coin knocking against a glass.

Reaching over, he switched on his bedside lamp and looked at the clock.

'2.30 a m. who could it be at this hour?' he thought to himself crossly.

Hoping it was not a death or a serious accident, he rose up quickly from his bed, threw on his dark blue wool dressing gown and hurried downstairs.

Switching on the outside light he opened the front door nervously. In the beam of light, and with his eyes still heavy from sleep, he found it hard to recognize the dark figure standing in the doorway.

'Yes,' he said quietly,' can I help you?'

'Willie it's me,' came a whispered reply.

Switching on the hall light, William looked again at his visitor. This time he knew the face but not the voice.

'Is there something wrong Harry?' he asked worriedly.

'Yes there is, can I come in? '

'Of course,' said William, stepping back and holding the door for his friend.

As Fr. Ferris stepped into the hall William closed the door behind him. Noticing his unfamiliar shabby appearance, William led the way into the large sitting room and switched on a small table lamp.

'Sit down there now and I'll get this fire going.' he said, motioning to a chair.

William knelt down and took the poker in his hand and began stoking up the dying embers. Then he threw some fresh sods of turf on it. Replacing the poker in its holder, he pulled up another chair opposite Fr. Ferris and sat down.

He was about to ask what the matter was, when he noticed great fear on the unshaven face sitting before him.

'I've been found out Willie.' said the other priest nervously,.

'Found out? What do you mean?' asked William looking rather puzzled.

'Found out with the boys.'

'What boys?'

Looking shamefaced down at the floor his friend replied: 'Altar boys.'

There was a stunned silence for a few minutes.

As William suddenly realised what his friend was saying, he put his two hands up to the top of his head in bewilderment.

'Oh God no, Harry, I don't believe this.' he said as his mind took in the horror of it.

'Willie don't look at me like that. Please, I need your help.'

Reeling from the shock, William suddenly rose from his chair. He was quite overcome, and this together with tiredness made him shiver. Running his fingers through his thick greying hair, he began to pace up and down the room.

Then he sat down directly across from the other priest and asked seriously:

'How Harry? How could you do such a despicable thing?'

Harold shuffled uneasily in his armchair.

'I really don't know,' he said, clearing his throat and looking down at his hands. 'I have tried to go back to when it first started and all I know is it started so easy. One morning I went into the vestry and one of the altar boys was crying because his Granny had died. I got down on my hunkers and hugged the wee lad. He hugged me back. His young soft cheek felt so good against mine.

He held on to my neck, and suddenly I realized how intensely I needed his touch. William you must know what I mean. Even his tears felt good against my skin.'

Then shaking his head he said embarrassingly:

'This is so hard,' and he scrunched his tormented eyes up tightly.

'I know,' said William,' But if I am to help I must know everything.'

'Over the next day or two I found myself thinking about him, wondering what he was at during the day. Then I started thinking about him at night, wondering if he had gone asleep yet. I even wondered if he had said his prayers. Then I found myself looking forward to being alone with him. I would touch him playfully on the head or on his soft cheeks. William you should have seen the trust in his innocent eyes when he looked at me.'

Burying his face in his big hands, Harold rubbed his skin worriedly. Then taking a deep sigh he went on,

'One morning I started tickling him and he wriggled and laughed and seemed to be enjoying it. Then one evening he called to my house. I brought him down to the kitchen and gave him some jelly and custard. I gave him a small bit first and then asked if he wanted more. The excitement I saw in his bright eyes as he said, 'Yes please' it caused a strange arousement to build up inside me.

I tried to ignore my feelings but they got stronger and would not go away. Then we went into the office to get the raffle tickets he had come for. While I was checking them at the table he stood very close watching me.

I could feel the heat of his body through my trousers. Before I knew what happened I was blinded by a rising passion and I…touched him. When the excitement died down I gave him some sweets and told him not to tell. Then I sent him home. I decided that night not to be alone with him again.'

Harold began wringing his hands, stood up and walked worriedly over to the window. Pulling back the curtains he looked out into the darkness for a few moments and then continued:

'As time went by I found myself longing for him. It became like a drug. I began to think up ways of getting him on his own. Then one evening after a football match, I offered to bring him home instead of letting him catch the bus. As he sat beside me in the car I suddenly wanted more than just touching.'

At this point in the story, William's forehead became very wrinkled and his stomach felt sick. He wished he could just get up and walk from the room. He did not want to hear any more of this. He felt a great evil creeping in between the two of them, and he was immediately repulsed by it.

But although he physically wanted to leave his spirit remained strong and he stayed.

Then he braced himself for anything else that Harold might say next.

'When it was over I gave him more sweets and some money and told him again to tell no one as they would not understand. From then on I found it easier to approach other boys. First the smaller ones, then the bigger ones.'

William leaned forward and placed his elbows on his knees.

'But Harry, did you not see the pain you were inflicting on these children. Did you not see the harm you were doing?' he asked raising his voice.

'But you don't understand, it was their fault, they tempted me. Sometimes I even thought they were enjoying it and sometimes I thought I felt a response.'

William was shocked even more by this remark and did not know what to say.

'But you must have known it was wrong,' he said again.

'No, it was like I was two people. Looking back on it now, I think I was two people. I never let the priest know what the man was doing.'

As Fr. Ferris sat looking into the glow of the fire he tried to explain his dreadful behaviour, Father William's face grew paler and at first he found it hard to listen. Instead he tried to fight back the anger that was building inside him. But then as Harold's words began to get through to him, he felt a desperate repulsion. He felt it so deeply that it stopped him from feeling compassionate towards his friend. So, instead of reaching out his hand in consolation, he walked over to the sideboard and poured out a stiff brandy.

Fr. Ferris shakily took the welcome drink from William's outstretched arm.

William knew his friend was deep in a sin that he never dreamt he would commit. Suddenly conflicting thoughts began tossing about in William's mind.

Finding he was unable to divide the sinner from the sin, unfamiliar feelings of hate rose up inside him.

In the moments that followed he did not know if they were aimed at his friend or what he had done. William clenched his fists and, for the first time in his life, felt almost uncontrollable anger. Only for the nobleness of his character and years of self- discipline restraining him, he felt he could hit out at his friend. But instead he walked to the other side of the room and struggled hard to hold the fury that surged through him.

As he calmed down a bit he glanced over at the black marble clock on the mantelpiece. Realising it was getting very late, he quickly decided to use the hour as an excuse to give him time to think. He also felt that with both of them now being in a state it would be better to deal with this in the morning.

'Harry,' he said,' I think we should leave this for now. The bed in the spare room is made up. You're very tired and upset so I think it's best we talk about this after we've both had some sleep.'

'I suppose you're right,' said Harold wearily as he swallowed the last of his drink.

Walking over to the fire, William placed the brass guard in front of it.

Fr. Ferris stood up slowly from his chair and put his glass down on a small table. After switching off the lights, the two priests walked quietly up the stairs.

On the landing William stopped and opened the hot press. Then, reaching in, he took out a pair of his own pyjamas. As he passed the warm clean clothes into Harold's outstretched hands a strange shiver went through him He suddenly became acutely aware of the impurity and evil of what his friend did. Then they both turned and went in different directions to their rooms

As the doors closed slowly behind them, the two priests were unaware that light and darkness were about to commence a demonic battle, and that all Heaven would praying.

Chapter 16.

Closing the door of his bedroom, Fr. William sat down wearily on the side of his bed. By now the tiredness had left him and he could not think of rest. In the silence that filled the room he could not believe all he had heard in the last hour.

Leaning forward, he rested his elbows on his knees, and dropped his face into his cupped hands. Closing his eyes tightly he stared into the private darkness of his own thoughts. A thousand questions gave way to flashing images.

These images were conjured up by the memories of Harold as a young student with him in the seminary.

A young man of medium height, Harold was inclined to shortness. His round head was a mass of thick wavy brown hair. His eyebrows were thick and straight with his long fringe hanging slightly over one of his dark eyes. His high cheekbones made his face appear quite chubby and two slightly prominent teeth gave him a most endearing smile. His light heartedness suited his personality and he had a great sense of fun.

Having been ordained together, the two friends were then dispatched to parishes that were at opposite ends of the country. Over the years they were delighted when they met up at retreats or special masses.

But now, these happy memories were being taken over by the horror of what had been revealed to William a little while ago. The thoughts of what Harold had inflicted on those innocent boys caused him to suddenly jump to his feet. Once again he clenched his fists in profound anger.

'How could he?' he asked himself,' after all we went through together. He wasn't just a friend, he was my confidante. The discussions, the prayers we shared, I thought we were of the same mind.'

Walking over to the window, he pulled back the curtains and looked out into the bleak night. Leaning wearily on the window frame, a great sadness came over him. With a sudden urge to get out of the house, William walked quickly to the door, opened it and hurried down the stairs. Removing his dressing gown, he took his overcoat from the hall tand and walked quickly through the front door.

A look of inexpressible distress had come over his usual calm face.

Pulling his collar up protectively around his neck he walked with long strides down the avenue. Even though the moon was full, the darkness beneath the trees seemed impenetrable.

With only the shadows for company, his felt loneliness and isolation in what now was going to be for him a very long night. His anger began to die down a little, and it was slowly being replaced by an icy fear that was twice as dangerous. Then, inside his mind a great struggle of faith began.

As Divine Grace came to reassure and calm him, so evil doubts rose up to confuse and agitate him. In this distressed confusion William was extremely vulnerable. Mixed with great sadness and heavy fatigue, physical images of sin took hold in his mind and he became more troubled. He felt the arrogance of hell coming to claim back the souls he had helped. He saw the filth of the sins that had been loaded onto him by penitents in the confessional. Truth became mixed up with more lies, as the devil continued to try to penetrate his mind and make his thoughts more believable. Suddenly Father William felt as if hell was crowding around him. Holding his head tightly and almost protectively, between his two hands, he again remembered all the sins he had forgiven in the name of Jesus and he wondered.

Many fears suddenly rose up inside the troubled priest and he cried out wearily:

'The world is corrupt, evil is more powerful.'

Then looking up searchingly at the sky, he cried out for the first time to God in desperation and anger:

'Where were you when Harold needed you? Why did you not stop this dreadful thing? What was all the religious teaching and education for if it was to end like this?'

In William's frightened reasoning, goodness now suddenly appeared too meek and gentle compared to the aggressive force of evil. Tears of frustration welled up in his eyes as he whispered in despair.

'Oh Lord are we fighting a losing battle?'

Then suddenly the worst thought of his life entered his distressed mind.

'What if something dreadful was ahead, in store for himself?'

In that moment all confidence which he derived from his faith seemed to desert him, and his own vulnerability to sin became very real as he shivered. Suddenly looking fearfully to his right and his left, he felt the darkness of the night suffocating him. Wiping his eyes he turned quickly and made his way back to the safety of his house.

On entering the hall the heat of the room only agitated him more, as he removed his coat and replaced it with his dressing gown. Noticing the light on in the kitchen, he went down the hall to investigate. On entering, he saw Fr. Ferris sitting at the table with a mug of tea, still dressed in his clerical clothes. Neither man spoke, they just stared blankly at each other. Noticing the distress in his friend's face Fr. Ferris asked nervously.

'Cup of tea Willie?'

'Please,' William replied, disgusted with himself for his sudden lack of compassion. As he walked over and sat down at the far end of the table, Harold felt the hurt of the unfamiliar coldness in William's voice.

But pouring out the tea, he thoughtfully remembered that his friend did not take sugar.

Harold was the first one to break the awkward silence.

'Willie,' he said seriously,' I've decided to go back to face my accusers. I can understand how you feel towards me now, but before I go, will you do something for me... would you hear my confession?'

William kept his sad eyes lowered to the ground as he answered quietly,

'Harry, don't ask me.'

Without even offering to shake hands, Fr. Ferris stood up, and with his head bowed ashamedly, walked slowly from the kitchen. As William heard the heavy hall door close, he stood up and had a great urge to go after him. But the cold hardness of his heart was too strong and it prevented him.

As he sat back down wearily in the chair, how the devil laughed to see two catholic priests, specially chosen, now locked in a dreadful spiritual conflict.

Chapter 17.

When Fr. Breen walked into the dining room for breakfast on Wednesday morning he found Fr. William already seated at the table. Within minutes, Mrs. Stapleton, their housekeeper, was following behind with two plates of freshly scrambled eggs. Placing the plates in front of the two men, her small checking eyes ran quickly over the table. Satisfied that the priests had everything else they required she spoke in her usual practical way.

'Right then eat up and if yez want anythin' else ya know where I am.'

Then she turned for the door and closed it firmly behind her.

Thanking her, Fr. Breen took his white linen napkin out of its silver ring and gave it three little shakes. Then he lifted his small chin and tucked the napkin carefully under his tight collar. Shaking a generous amount of salt over his eggs, he picked up his fork and scooped up a small portion of the hot delicious yellow food. Then as he raised his cup to his mouth he watched William closely from underneath his eyes. The two men continued eating their meal in almost total silence.

A short while later, William, having finished his meal, excused himself, got up from the table and left the room.

He was just settled at his writing desk when the door of his study burst open and Fr. Breen marched in.

'Right William, this has gone far enough.'

William looked up surprised. 'What's gone far enough Dan?'

'You. There has been no living with you for the last few weeks. I'm fed up with the way you've been moping around the place. Even Orla is worried about you. Have we done something on you?'

'No, not at all,' answered William quickly, but the tone of his voice did not convince Fr. Breen.

'Look, I know there is something wrong, are you in some kind of trouble? Did anything happen to you in Liverpool?'

'No, no,' William assured him.

'Well for God sake,' the older priest said getting agitated, 'stop acting like a schoolboy and tell me what's wrong. I'm not living like this much longer.'

William heard the determination in the older priest's voice to get to the bottom of it, and he knew he would have to give him an explanation. So sitting back in his chair, he rested his hands in his lap and began:

'It happened the night I came back from England. It was a friend of mine from our days in the seminary.' another long pause.

'Well what about him?'

'He called here late that night and he was in very serious trouble.' another pause.

'What sort of trouble?' asked Fr. Breen as he folded his arms.

William rose from the desk and walked over to the window. In a low voice he said hesitantly,

'He has been accused of abusing some boys.'

'I see,' said Fr. Breen, sitting down in William's place, 'This **is** serious.'

'I'm afraid it is,' said William worriedly.

'I wonder who reported him?' thought Fr. Breen as he scratched his head curiously.

'Well, when Harry left here the other night he was going to back to face the situation.'

Turning from the window, William walked over to a table and leaned hard on it. When he went to speak the words came rushing out.

'I just could not believe when he told me. I was so disgusted and betrayed. I suppose because we were so close I thought I knew him. We had such great discussions, so much in common.'

Fr. Breen turned round in his chair.

'And how did you get on with him the night he called here?' he asked

'I'm afraid I handled it very badly,' admitted William, walking up and down the room.

'In what way did you do that?' Fr. Breen asked curiously.

'Well, I suppose I was so disgusted at what he did that I found it hard to show him any compassion.'

Picking up a silver letter opener, Fr. Breen fiddled with it.

'Yes William, I imagine you would,' he said quietly.

'I couldn't help it, I was never so angry.'

'But why did you get angry?'

William was unable to answer. In the silence that followed Fr. Breen stared hard at him.

'Have you ever been seriously tempted William?' he asked bluntly.
'No, of course not,' he said irritably.
'Have you ever wanted for anything?'
'No,'
'Of course you haven't. Everything you ever wanted was handed to you. You had the best of education, clothes, holidays, even a new car all handed to you. What do you know about life? Take the other night for example. The first time you came up against a real crisis you couldn't cope. You were arrogant.' As William went on to defend himself and tell the details of that night, the latter listened very carefully. When he had finished, Fr. Breen pushed the chair back from the desk and looked up seriously at his curate.

'Why didn't you wake me ?' he asked seriously.

William looked puzzled and gave no reply.

'A priest called looking for help, you were confronted with a very serious problem. As well as being terrible for the priest involved, it will have repercussions on the faithful and the catholic church. You could not deal with it yourself and did you not think I could have helped? '

'But it was very late and I didn't want to disturb you,' replied William as he tried to explain his behaviour.

'Why, is there a sign on my door saying I'm not to be disturbed? Since when is God's work nine to five?'

'I suppose I wasn't thinking, in fact I could not think at all.'

Fr. Breen looked into William's sad eyes and said firmly:

'Because it was your friend you couldn't deal with this, but I could have helped that man.'

William tried to protest.

'No, let me finish,' said Fr. Breen crossly. 'I'm afraid you've had things too easy, you've been shielded from the real world far too long. You think you've all the answers but let me tell you now Father, you don't even know the questions.'

'That's not true' protested William

Father Breen's face took on a very high colour. Angrily he stood up and walked over beside his curate.

'So far this conversation has been all about you and how you felt.' he said, lowering his voice. 'How distressed and how angry you were. Damn it William, One of Gods children came to this house looking for help. He should have got it. It doesn't matter what he did. We do not set ourselves up as judge and jury.'

Suddenly William was shocked as he realised that the older priest was right.

'I'm sorry but I have to say this,' continued Fr. Breen as he rose from the chair, when you came here, suddenly the church wasn't big enough, or should I say not grand enough for you. Then you wanted to get too involved with the people. They're not that well off, but still you put pressure on them to build a new church. Then you decided that we didn't need two houses, that we only needed one. Now, you think about it, you went to the Bishop over my head and got his support. Sometimes I think you built that church as a monument to yourself?'

'God no, 'protested William,

Fr. Breen walked over and opened the door. 'You are a good priest William,' he said kindly,' but I think you have an awful lot to learn. Now I want you to snap out of this mood your in immediately and get back to your duties.'

As he went to leave the room he suddenly turned back.

'You know,' he said thoughtfully,' there are only two things in this world that really scare me, that is a young priest and an old doctor, neither of them know how to listen.'

Chapter 18.

With Fr. William having returned to Ireland, Molly went about her nursing duties in the English hospital as usual. By now the bed at the window in 'ward ten' had a new patient in it, and often times Molly would catch herself looking sadly over at it.

The following evening she was about to go off duty, when her friend Pat told her she was wanted on the office phone.

Picking up the receiver she was surprised to hear Edgar Archer on the other end. He had rung to say he was now going to open another insurance office in Liverpool and would like to meet her again.

Suddenly the tiredness left her as her eyes lit up with excitement. With her heart beating faster, she eagerly agreed. Then, after replacing the receiver, she glided as if with wings under her feet, back to the Nurses Home.

Hurrying into her room, she picked up her ABBA album and put it on the record player. Then, as the strains of the first song filled the air, she hurriedly skipped the needle over to her favourite track, 'The day before you came.' For the next few hours Molly pulled out all her clothes from the wardrobe, trying to decide what to wear. Soon the news of her important date spread among her friends. Getting caught up in the romance of it all, they took turns sitting on her bed and offering their advice.

The next day Molly's excitement reached an even higher level but the afternoon seemed to go so slow. She had a creak in the back of her neck from constantly looking down at her fob watch to check the time. But eventually when five o clock came, all that could be seen of Nurse Furlong was her navy cape flying high behind her as she raced across the hospital grounds. At six forty-five she was ready and waiting in the hall.

Looking particularly lovely, with her long thick black hair showing off the white of her short cotton dress. Enhanced by tiny flowers woven into the fabric, it fitted her slim figure like a glove. She wore very little makeup as her clear white skin had a beauty all of its own.

On the dot of five-thirty a silver Jaguar car pulled up at the door. As Molly walked down the steps, Edgar stood holding the passenger door open for her.

'You look beautiful,' he said smiling, as he closed the door behind her.

Then slipping easily into the driver's seat he turned on the engine and they headed towards town.

On the journey many feelings rose up inside Molly. She was in awe of his beautiful car but shy of his many questions. She felt inadequate of his designer clothes, but was impressed with his knowledge of business. The smell of his after-shave seemed to smother her less expensive scent, but whenever he turned, smiled or reached for her hand, her spirits lifted and all these other things were forgotten.

Arriving at the Tower restaurant he walked behind her as they went through the doors. Running his hand down her shiny hair she heard him say in his perfect English accent:

'It is beautiful.'

In that moment Molly felt like a queen.

As they enjoyed their delicious dinner of lamb and duck, she began to relax and leave the whole evening in his capable hands.

From that night on Molly's life took on a rather dreamlike state. She was bowled over, not just by his manners, but by his smooth conversation and his wonderful sense of style. She sometimes felt honoured that of all the girls he knew, he chose to be with her.

He introduced her to a whole different world when they visited more expensive restaurants and gambling casinos. Molly would stand in amazement watching him throw a small fortune away.

'That is my entire wages for the month,' she whispered as he calmly pushed the notes through a slit in the gambling table.

But Edgar took her hand and only laughed when he saw the shocked look on her face.

'Don't worry darling,' he said casually, 'there's plenty more where that came from.'

As the weeks passed the young couple began to see much more of each other. Edgar transferred to Liverpool and bought himself a house. Pretty soon his silver Jag was a familiar sight parked outside the nurses home. Before long they became known as 'an item.'

Molly was so impressed by his sophisticated voice and his gentlemanly ways. He took up all her thoughts and everything she did was with him in mind. Never had Molly Furlong been in love like this before. So it was only to be expected that when, after a show in the theatre some time later, that Edgar proposed and Molly whole heatedly accepted.

'Yes I will marry you,' she said, as he slid the large diamond ring on her the fourth finger of her left hand.

Her thoughts were immediately filled with the wonderful big family wedding she had always dreamed of.

Later when she was alone in her room she lay in bed staring up at the ceiling. It was all so much like a fairytale. As she fiddled with the beautiful ring on the fourth finger of her left hand she thought about all the love she wanted to give this wonderful man. A lot of what he had said made sense and it really pleased her that he was so romantic. But still little doubts played on her mind.

'I know I'll ring home first thing in the morning,' she thought to herself.' I'll ask Aunt Hattie's advice about the wedding.'

But then after thinking some more, Molly decided it was time she let go of Hattie's apron strings and made a few decisions herself.

Chapter 19.

Having finished up in the dairy, Walter Furlong and his faithful dog Shep, went up to the top field to check on the single suckler herd. As Walter strolled through the fields he carefully opened and closed each gate behind him. Looking down at the thick mud on his boots he began thinking back to the evening before. It had rained heavy all day, and having done the necessary jobs around the farm, he decided to leave the rest until the skies cleared. Frank had gone to Wexford town early that morning and was not expected back until dark. After dinner, the rain continued to lash down outside, while Hattie and Walter sat at the fire in the warm kitchen. They reminisced about old times, and as they did their parents and that had passed away came alive again in their emotional conversation.

After a while Hattie got up to make the tea.

'Hold off with yer tea now sis,' said Walter winking mischievously. Rising from his chair, he hurried from the kitchen. Puzzled as to what he was up to, Hattie remained seated. In a few moments he returned with two glasses in one hand and a bottle of sherry and a bottle of whisky in the other.

'It's a bit early for that don't you think?' she asked seriously.

Walter exaggerated his movements as he looked up at the old clock.

'No better time,' he replied smiling,' come on sis let yer hair down for once.'

Hattie smiled to herself as she remembered her times with Nicholas.

'Well,' she said innocently, straightening her skirt, 'I suppose one won't do any harm, but we would not want to make a habit of this.'

'That's it,' said Walter happily, as he began pouring.

The evening wore on and they laughed and laughed remembering things they had both forgotten. Walter at one stage, on hearing a familiar tune on the radio, got up from his seat and did a little waltz on the floor.

He did it for no other reason than to prove that he was still the best dancer in Wexford. Hattie smiled at his lively efforts and clapped her hands in amusement. But then, suddenly noticing her brother getting a little breathless, her mood quickly changed.

'Sit down or you'll get a heart attack,' she said worriedly, reaching forward to catch him.

Walter laughed as he did what he was told, stopped dancing telling her not to be fussing. Then he went over to the table and topped up his drink. Sitting back in his chair he sighed heavily, then slowly his smile faded from his lips.

'I miss her ya know Hattie,' he said sadly, 'after all these years I still miss my Doris.'

'Yes I know,' said Hattie sympathetically as she remembered her late sister- in- law.

The mood in the kitchen suddenly changed to a more sombre one. Then Hattie began thinking about her late husband James.

Suddenly James was taken over by the memory of Nicholas Robinson, as his handsome smiling face flashed before her eyes.

'Yes you'd know, Hattie,' continued Walter as he looked into the fire,' Because there's two things you and me have in common, one is that we both reared good family's single-handed, and we both found and lost true love. You with James, me with Doris.'

Hattie suddenly realised that Walter really had no idea just how much Nicholas had meant to her.

With the drink now beginning to take effect, he continued to ramble on and on about James. It was only now Hattie realized that the love she felt for Nicholas must have been invisible to Walter. Of course she would never have told how deep her feelings were unless she was going to make a commitment, and sadly, with Nicholas's circumstances she never could.

So putting her memories back in that special place in her mind, she changed the subject. Knowing how lonely her brother was for his late wife, she began conjuring up little things she remembered about the petite gentle woman who, in her short life, had given her brother so much happiness.

As Walter listened his eyes took on a loving glazed expression and once or twice a tear welled up in his old eyes. When Hattie had finished he stood up, took her by the hand, and led her to the sitting room.

Lifting the lid of their late mother's piano, he asked if she would play something for him. Hattie willingly obliged and sitting upright on the stool began her rendering of 'Beethoven's Moonlight Sonata'.

As the first chords filled the air Walter sat down and listened. He watched Hattie closely. She was very dear to him too. He had played with her as a child, teased her as a teenager, was proud of her elegance and pleased with her choice of partner in marriage.

Now, in the twilight of her years, he looked fondly on her greying hair and fading beauty and, for the first time in a long while Walter Furlong realized just how precious it was to have a sister.

But today, strolling among the cows, Walter gave a little chuckle. He remembered with great fondness the fun they both had in that lovely long evening of yesterday.

Suddenly he heard the thunder of hooves behind him. Thinking it was one of the cows chasing the dog he did not turn round. But then when the dog barked loudly Walter turned immediately. To his horror he saw the Friesian bull coming straight for him. There was no time to run. In his panic, he frantically waved his arms and stick in the air while shouting loudly. But to no avail, the bull kept charging. Then, with all the force of a cannon ball, the large beast pucked the top of his hard head straight into Walter's stomach.

Without time to even utter a prayer Walter Furlong was dead.

Then, unaware of the sacredness of it, the bull lifted his weightless body up off the ground and tossed it forward. Then he began playing with it as if it was a rag doll.

Shep continued barking and running at the bull. Snapping his jaws viciously, he managed to bite him hard on the heels. Feeling the sting, the bull momentarily forgot his plaything and lashed out once more. With powerful force he hurled the dog back on the ground. In a second Shep lay very still and silent, his small neck broken.

Then the bull went over and once more pucked at Walter's body. Snorting frantically through his nostril's he angrily pawed the ground. Then eventually, he stopped and stood triumphantly over his kill.

The herd of cows, completely unmoved by the carnage, grazed away down the field. The bull stood quietly for a further twenty minutes between the body and the herd and then he too moved unaffectedly away to join them.

Meanwhile, back in the yard, Frank went around the outhouses calling for the Boss. Getting no reply, he went indoors and asked Hattie if she had seen him.

'No,' she replied,' but sur, he'll be in shortly. I'm ready to put the dinner on the table and you know your father, he never misses his meals.'

But Frank continued to look worried.

'I've an awful feelin' there's somethin' wrong,' he said, scratching his head and looking out the window.

'But sure what could be wrong? Now come and get your dinner, he'll be in a minute.'

Frank sat in at the table, but half way through the meal he put his knife and fork down.

'Did the Boss say he was goin' anywhere?'

'No, he said nothing to me,' replied Hattie.

Frank pushed his chair back and got up from the table.

'Stick my dinner in the oven, I'm goin'out to find him,' he said as he walked out the door, across the yard and up the fields.

Looking down at the soft ground he noticed boot and paw prints in the mud. He knew now what direction the Boss had taken. Whistling for Shep, he headed into the top field. Hurrying along anxiously, he saw what looked like a coat lying on the ground. Then he noticed the Friesian bull throwing his head in the air. Suddenly the bull ran towards him. Frank turned, ran like hell and just barely made it over the gate as the animal skidded to a halt behind him.

Climbing up on the pillars, he looked out across the field. Realising what must have happened, at the same time he desperately hoped he was wrong. Then, with his eyes glued to the coat, he had a great urge to get back into the field. But having a fear of the bull he hesitated, and thought for a few minutes.

Running faster now, he got back to the yard in a matter of minutes and staggered to the tractor. Climbing in quickly, he started the engine and headed back to the field.

As he approached he saw the bull standing about fifty yards from the coat. Getting out of the tractor, he hurried to open the gate. Driving on, he suddenly noticed Shep lying motionless in the grass. Then looking over fearfully at the coat, he suddenly realised it was the body of his father.

As Frank stopped the tractor the bull charged but then skidded to a halt. Then he stood roaring and pawing the ground. Ignoring him, Frank braked, dropped the transporter box attached to the back, and inched it up carefully to the body. Climbing out the back, he quickly rolled Walter's body into the transport box, while all the time keeping a careful eye on the bull. Then he climbed back in, rose up the box, and drove over to where the dog lay. Repeating the dreadful procedure, he rolled the dog on to his masters feet. Then he drove carefully out of the field and back to the farmyard, stopping only once to shut the gate.

Back at the farmhouse Hattie found that she too had no appetite. Frank had her all worried now. So, covering her dinner with a plate, she went over and placed it in the oven beside the others. Then she kept a serious watch at the kitchen window.

When Frank drove into the yard a little while later, Hattie saw Shep's tail hanging from the box. As she hurried out the back door Frank failed to get out of the tractor fast enough to stop her seeing the rest.

Running over to the box, she let out a sudden gasp when she saw Walter's battered body huddled inside and all covered in muck.

Clutching her chest, she leaned forward and fought hard to prevent feelings of nausea from rising inside her. The terrible shock caused her to stagger, and Frank just managed to prevent her from falling.

'Come away,' he said sadly, 'there's nothing we can do.'

'Ah Lord, Walter what happened to you?' she asked in a shaking voice as she broke free from Frank's arms.

'It was the bull,' replied Frank,' he's gone mad, we may ring for the vet.'

Not hearing his words, Hattie walked over to the other side of the transport box. Taking her white handkerchief from her sleeve, she began to wipe the muck away from her brothers lovely silver hair.

'Ah Walter,' she cried again.

For the first time in years, since that day he told her she could not have Doireann, she felt that the bridges between them were mended. Frank tried to pull her away but she held on even more tightly to her beloved brother and would not let go.

'Right,' he said quietly, 'I'll go in and make the phone calls, I won't be a minute.' With that he ran quickly into the house.

Hattie continued stroking her brother's body tenderly and between moans and tears her heart began to break. Bending over, she strained to kiss his face. Then Frank returned from the house with a blanket.

He told Hattie he had phoned Doireann and David and told them the bad news. Handing her the blanket, he said|:

'You cover the Boss, I'll remove the dog.'

'Ah poor Shep,' said Hattie, 'isn't this dreadful?'

Picking it up in his arms, Frank carried the dog across the yard and laid it down on some dry hay in front of the hay shed.

Meanwhile no mother ever covered a child as carefully as Hattie covered her Walter. She tucked the blanket tightly in behind and all around him. Then, with just his pale mud-stained face exposed, she continued stroking his hair. Despite Frank's persuading she would did leave him until the priest came.

A little while later Fr. Murphy arrived on the tragic scene. He gave Walter the last rites of his faith. Then he reverently covered the rest of the body with the blanket and went inside to ring for an ambulance.

Frank put his arm around Hattie and felt her trembling.

'Why don't you go in and warm yourself, there's nothing more we can do now,' he said sadly.

Hattie was about to refuse when she looked up at Frank and noticed how dreadfully pale he was. It was only now she realised the shock her nephew must have got.

'I'll go in and make us both some strong tea,' she said looking back sadly.

In the hours that followed, the yard at big house never had so much traffic on its cracked concrete. First the ambulance arrived to take Walters body away for a post mortem. Then, as the news spread, neighbours and friends came to offer assistance. Frank was very grateful when they helped him round up and bring the herd of cattle into the pen. Then, after a bit of a struggle, they managed to get the bull into the testing chute. As the vet gave it an anaesthetic, Frank could not help thinking angrily that it was more than the Boss got. The herd was then let back out into the field while the killer bull was loaded into a lorry and sent off to the meat factory.

Inside the house Hattie was kept busy overseeing the preparations for the wake. That night Walter Furlong returned for the last time to his beloved Riversdale. As he lay cold in the coffin, Hattie looked over at the piano in the corner. She remembered the fun and the singing of yesterday evening.

'Oh Maureen,' she said sadly, 'It couldn't be a coincidence that we felt so close before he died.'

Once more she cried bitterly. Lady Gowne went over and put her arms around her and tried to comfort her.

By now most of the family had gathered with neighbours and friends.

Doireann walked slowly over to her father's remains. Reaching over, she touched his hands.

Oh how well she knew those hands, every line and scar. As a child she often sat watching him eating his meals or making things. Suddenly she noticed the split in his thumb nail. Smiling, she remembered the day he came into the kitchen calling the hammer all the names he could think of. Then, it was their size and strength that caught her attention. However in later years, it was his gentle touch that made her feel protected and loved.

But now, as she felt their marble-like texture and their unfamiliar coldness, a great sense of loss struck at her heart. She cried uncontrollably. Garrett, standing by her side, wished he could do something to spare her all this. Reaching over he tried to comfort her by gently massaging the side of her neck.

David, her brother, had stood broken-hearted in the same place a little while before. But needing to be alone, he had left the house and gone walking up to the fields.

Leaning forward on the gate, he looked out across top field. The beautiful green mystical landscape gave no sign of the violence that had been acted out on it in the last few hours. It was only now, away from the mourning crowd that David could let go. In this solitude a great heaviness descended on him. The sudden great loss of his father caused his head to bend and his shoulders to heave with great sadness. He thought of how the Boss had reared the bull from a calf and how proud he was of him. How often he had heard him say that the animal was from a good line. But then little did any of them know the same bull would turn out to be a killer.

Roaring now from the depths of his being, David, in his dreadful grief, recognised the same agonizing pain in his heart that he had felt many years before, at the death of his beloved Molly. As time passed he did not know for which of them he was crying. As his tears gave way to deep sobbing his head began to throb and his throat felt dry.

Standing up, he looked out once more across the top field and saw the herd grazing as usual. Then suddenly an uplifting thought entered his mind.

'Wasn't this the land the Boss had lived for? The place he had taken his first and last breath.'

The more David thought about it, the more calm and consoled he became. His Father had died on the land and deep down David knew that the Boss would not have been happy dying anywhere else.

It was in the early hours of the following morning that Frank left the family praying and went quietly outside. The memory of the terrible carnage he had witnessed now seemed suspended in the stillness of the morning air. Feeling a little light-headed and weary, he walked slowly over to the hay shed. Bending down sadly, he picked the dead dog up by his paws. Then he took the spade and walked out into the orchard. There, he dug a deep hole and buried his faithful friend. As he patted the brown clay with the back of the spade, for the first time since the awful tragedy, he broke down.

'Oh Shep,' he cried, as he looked helplessly at the grave.

From a short distance behind one of the apple trees a young woman stood watching.

She watched motionless as Frank's pain and grief reached an insufferable level. Then she turned slowly hoping to steal away. Suddenly her foot snapped a large twig. On hearing the sound Frank wiped his wet eyes quickly. Then, looking embarrassingly around, he caught sight of a figure hurrying away. He knew immediately who it was, and the reason Frank Furlong knew, was, he had never stopped loving her.

Chapter 20.

Two days later as the mourners filed into St Anne's Church in Wexford some of them could not understand why there were two coffins placed in front of the altar. In the vestry Father William sat with his head bowed. His mind went over and over it and still he, too, found it all hard to believe.

On receiving the tragic news of his uncle's death, he went immediately to be with his mother. On the journey from Laois he worried about how all this would affect her. But when he arrived she just lit another cigarette and said she was fine. Looking at her red eyes and drawn features he was unconvinced. Continuing to show his concern, Hattie insisted that he stop fussing. So instead he set about comforting the rest of the family who were in a dreadful state of turmoil.

Been given special leave by the hospital, Molly flew in from Liverpool that morning. Having a great impulse to tell everyone about her engagement, the shock and sorrow that greeted her on her arrival made her refrain from doing so. On entering the kitchen she saw Hattie standing at the cooker in floods of tears. Dropping her bags, she ran over and put her arms around her. As the two women hugged, Molly discreetly removed her engagement ring and closed her hand tightly on it. Hattie cried as if her heart would break. At the same time Seamus and Eithne drove into the yard. From the back of the car their children looked out curiously through the windows.

Going between family, friends and neighbours William felt his efforts to bring peace and calm to the situation were in vain. For once he felt totally useless. The shock and sorrow of his uncle's sudden death was just too great. So when his mother asked him to go into town and collect Julie from the bus he was relieved to get away for awhile. He decided to take his young nephews and nieces for the drive. On the journey their innocent chatter and constant giggling cheered his sad heart.

As always, he was amazed how children seemed to live in a world of their own, which was so different from the pressures and sadness of grown ups.

When the bus pulled in he was glad to see Julie. On the way back to the house he suggested that she might talk to his mother and persuade her to rest.

'Well you know your mother is not one to take orders,' said Julie quiet seriously. But then she quickly promised she would try.

'We'll be going out in a minute to say the Mass,' whispered Fr. Breen as he interrupted William's thoughts, 'are you sure you're up to it?'

William looked over at the five priests who had come to express their sympathy and concelebrate the Mass with him, and he gave them a half smile.

'Yes I'm fine,' he said unconvincingly.

Fr. Breen touched his hand supportively and returned to talk to his companions. William remained seated and once more found his thoughts going over the events of yesterday.

As the sun rose over 'Riversdale House' a strange sad tiredness had come over the occupants. It had been a long night, with the adult members of the family staying up to pray for Walter's soul.

The next morning William was sitting at the table having some breakfast while Julie and Hattie were standing at the sink washing the dishes. Mind you they were not just ordinary dishes, it was Hattie's best china tea set

She had cornered Julie earlier and told her that she was the only one to be trusted with such an important task. So, as they stood together at the sink, Hattie gave the full history of where she got them, and how long she had them. Julie in turn was able to remember the wonderful occasions that they had used them. As William sat listening to them chatting away he could not help thinking it was like old times. He too remembered the tea set from his childhood, but in those days, and with other things on his mind, he would not have taken much stock of the crockery.

Walking over to the sink, he stood beside his mother and took one of the delicate cups in his hands. Holding it up to the light he inspected it closely. As he began to see the beauty in the detail of the hand-painted pattern, it was only now he knew what she was talking about. He also became aware of the great respect she had for the things she loved.

After washing and rinsing each delicate piece separately, Julie carefully passed them into Hattie's hands. In turn she dried them with a soft white tea towel, and then just as carefully placed them on a large silver tray beside her.

As Julie passed the last cup over to her, Hattie suddenly turned and looked up thoughtfully at William.

'You probably think I'm mad going on about this china but it's one of the few things I've left from the time with your father,' she said affectionately.

William smiled, bent down and kissed her cheek,

'No Mother I don't think you're mad, I think you're wonderful,' he said, smiling.

Her eyes lit up as she smiled back at him.

Then handing him the tea towel she picked up the tray and said seriously:

'I want to put these back in the cabinet in case they get broken. William, will you follow me with the teapot?'

As he turned to take the tray for her, she suddenly dropped to the floor sending the precious tea set crashing.

'Mother,' he shouted as he knelt down beside her.

Within seconds Seamus, Molly and Doireann had appeared from the sitting room.

'What's happened?' they asked worriedly.

'She just fell down.' said Julie in a shocked voice.

Then, with shaking hands, she quickly bent down to pick up the pieces of china which lay scattered all over the floor.

Carefully lifting Hattie's head, William asked worriedly:

'Are you alright mother?' But there was no reply.

Seamus reached over quickly and taking her hand, felt for a pulse.

Then bending even further down, he straightened her body out on the floor and began to resuscitate her, but getting no response in the next few crucial minutes, he gave up, and shook his head hopelessly. Their mother was dead.

Dropping down hard on his knees William lifted her head as his gentle heart shattered. Holding her in his arms, it was only now, as she lay subdued in death, that he dared take her small precious face in his hands. As he caressed and looked at the kind features that had always loved him, his heavy tears fell silently. Feeling a desire to stroke her hair, he gently pressed his cheek down on hers and in an instant the familiar scent of her skin brought him back to his childhood. He remembered sitting on her lap and she smiling down at him. Then his mind flashed to the day when he had seen her as a real woman. Oblivious to the rest of the family gathered round, he began to rock her protectively in the cradle of his arms. Then slowly a strange peace came over him as he thought:

'She is with God now.'

After a while Seamus touched his shoulder:

'Come away,' he said sadly, 'there's nothing we can do.'

As the cold realisation that their mother was dead began to sink in, William gently laid her down. Then, whispering a special prayer in her ear, he very reluctantly let her go.

Walking out on the altar now he looked down in disbelief at the two coffins lying side by side. He suddenly felt the whole thing was so unreal. It was only now that he deeply regretted not insisting more that his mother should rest.

Joining his hands, he looked down at the large congregation that had packed into the church. In the front row of seats sat two families completely devastated. The people he loved most in the world were sitting before him in floods of tears. So it was with a heavy heart that William, later on in the ceremony, stood up to speak about his uncle Walter and his beloved mother.

'It is hard for me to know where to start,' he began as he adjusted the microphone, 'because it's at times like this I can only feel. I had no time to prepare anything so I can only speak from my heart.'

Then, clearing his throat, he began:

'It was only yesterday that mother told me of the wonderful evening she and Walter shared the day before he was killed. She told me how they both laughed and shared happy memories on that special afternoon.'

Then pointing to the two coffins he continued sadly:

'I don't know why all this should have happened, but when they died, both of these wonderful people were doing what they had always done. Walter was walking the land and taking care of his stock, while mother, like any other was washing the dishes.'

Then, motioning to the two coffins, he continued:

'These people did not spend their lives chasing an illusion. To the very end they were true to what's real. This in itself is a tribute not only to the type of people they were, but to the families they came from.

Walter was a sound and honourable man. He was deeply loved by his children; David, Frank and Doireann and respected by neighbours and friends. But if I were to pay a tribute to him it would be this,

He set his own course in life and whether we thought he was right or wrong, he always had the courage and perseverance to stick to it.' Then William paused as he looked down at his mother's coffin.

The tears welled up in his eyes as with trembling lips he said proudly,

'If I were to think of one thing that would sum up the lady that was our mother, it is Hattie Thornton could never be less than she was.'

Then, taking his hankerchief from his pocket he wiped away his tears.

'As I look back on the great sadness of the last two days, there is one thing only that gives me consolation. I believe that the Divine Love, which deemed them worthy of life will now take them back as His own. I hope Walter will meet his beloved wife Doris, and that mother will meet our father James, and together they will spend many a happy evening in Heaven remembering and praying for us, their children.'

Then, with a shaking voice full of love, he concluded:

'Eternal rest grant unto to them Oh Lord, and may your perpetual light shine upon them, and may they rest in peace amen.'

Chapter 21.

Fr. William went about his duties by day but at night he could not sleep. His enormous sense of loss and grief was only added to by the home truths that Fr. Breen had coldly pointed out to him.

Memories, questions and recriminations continued to torment him his already troubled mind. He often rose from his bed, having only slept a little, to weep in the early hours of the morning. Sometimes he would cry so hard he felt his tears were cutting into his cheeks.

To suddenly realise that he was guilty, of among others, the great sin of pride tormented his soul. Everything he had done in good faith for his parish over the years came before him as bold acts of selfishness.

Through all his soul searching William's health began to suffer. His hearty appetite left him and he began to lose weight. This lack of nourishment, combined with little sleep, added to his depressed state. He began to believe that everything Fr. Breen had said was true.

Yes, he was from a privileged background and wanted for nothing. He had taken a vow of poverty at his ordination, and yet he had accepted a present of a new car. He often enjoyed eating in hotels, playing golf and going on holidays.

He eventually had to admit that his lifestyle was sometimes far removed from the gospels. But his mind argued that this was not entirely his fault. This was the way of life for most priests and without thinking he had gone along with it.

As the weeks went by William's self confidence became dangerously low. He could not think straight and no longer believed he had the ability to make proper decisions. The peace that he always took for granted deserted his soul and in the space that remained a dreadful struggle began. It was in this turmoil that William lost himself.

He became as if blind and had no sense of his own misery or his own worth. When celebrating the sacrifice of the Mass he just went through the motions. He was unable to enter into it with the faith that the presence of Jesus was actually on the altar. He found it much easier to think than to pray, and it was in one of these dark thoughts that William began to doubt he was ever fit to be a priest.

With Fr. Breen's indifference to the situation, Orla Stapelton decided enough was enough, it was time to take matters into her own hands.

The following week Fr. Thornton was called to the Bishop's Palace. An efficient looking secretary showed him into the Bishop's chambers. He could not help feeling a little puzzled as to why he had been summoned. Rising up from his knees after kissing the Bishop's ring, William was surprised to see a smile break out on his superior's usually stern face.

As he motioned him to sit down at his desk William asked anxiously:

'You wanted to see me your Grace?'

Without replying, Bishop Commins sat down in his large antique chair, opened a drawer on his right, then leaned across and placed a letter in front of William.

'I'd like you to read that Fr. Thornton.'

Taking his glasses case from his breast pocket, the first thing William noticed was the address at the top right hand side of the page. Then, recognizing the familiar uniform handwriting, William read the following.

The Presbytery,
Co, Laois.

Dear your Grace,

I know you're a very busy man and I don't like havin' to trouble you with me problems but I'm awful worried about young Fr. William.

Ya see yur grace its like this, it started the time he came back from Liverpool two months ago now. First I noticed he wouldn't finish the good food I put in front of him. Then he started pickin' at it, and now he keeps tellin' me he's not hungry. Your Grace I'm really worried because he's getting shockin' thin.

Now on top of that your Grace, he's up all hours of the night. His bed is hardly slept in. I do hear him wanderin' up and down the stairs openin' and shuttin' doors into the early hours of the mornin'. Sometimes he even goes outside in the dark, and lately he's started to leave lights on after him. I don't think he's in pain as there is no mention of a Doctor. So now I think the trouble is in his mind.

I've tried to talk to Fr. Breen about it but he has his own troubles.
I'm sorry to be botherin you yer Grace but I'm at me wits end with worry.
He's got shockin' thin and quiet.
I know you'll find out what's wrong sur he'd have to tell you,
                Yours faithfully
                Orla Stapleton, the housekeeper.

Fr. William finished the letter and replaced it on the desk. He shook his head slowly as a small smile broke out on his face. The Bishop joined his hands and sat back in his chair.

'Well that woman is right about two things William,' said the Bishop sternly, 'you have lost weight and you will have to tell me.'

As William recalled the shocking events of the night Harold called and his own reaction to it, the Bishop sat listening intently. He then went on to explain the home truths that Fr. Breen made him so aware of. He told of his fears and his subsequent loss of faith. Then with his eyes filling up with tears he finished by saying how lately he felt unworthy to be a priest.

When he had finished, the Bishop sat motionless in his chair. With his hands joined in his lap he thought deeply for a few moments. He knew William's soul was suffering and that that was far worse than his body. When he eventually spoke his voice softened but still retained a depth of seriousness.

'There is a time,' he began, 'when something dreadful comes into our lives and shatters our peace, but you know it's how we behave in that situation that is important. These emotions of anger, disgust and lack of compassion that you felt towards your friend, are not faults as long as they are under the control of your reason. But you must never let yourself be led by them. I must say though, I am very disappointed that you would let somebody like Fr. Breen undermine your self-confidence.'

'But I have been selfish in the past, coming to you with my plans,' replied William.

'On the contrary, may I say that your service to your parish over the years has been remarkable,' contradicted the Bishop.

Then he went on, 'You came to me from time to time, and having thought about your proposals, I was glad to give my approval. As regards going behind Fr. Breen's back you only asked permission, it was always my decision and only mine. Tell me something William, what did you ever ask for yourself?'

'Nothing.'

'What do you own?'

'My clothes and the car my mother bought me.'

'Exactly, and if you were given money in the morning what would you do with it?'

William smiled at the thoughts of such a concept and replied: Give it to the poor.'

The Bishop tapped the desk and once again said: 'Exactly.'

Thinking for a moment, William leaned over and protested:

'But you don't understand, I have been so full of pride.'

'So you keep telling me, but I disagree. Look, there will always be somebody to point out your faults. Never be upset by criticism receive it with humility and it will never upset you. When you pray, the more humble you are the more you will be fit to approach God. Anyway, anyone who sees self-confidence as arrogance has a big problem.'

'But you don't understand…'

'No it is you who doesn't understand,' interrupted the Bishop,

'Up to now you have heard the word of God and kept it. But lately you are beginning to feel its sting. Our whole life is a struggle and we are all soldiers of Christ. Therefore we must fight a good fight. Mind you, while some of us rise from the lowest depth to holiness, others can fall from Heaven to hell.'

'But your Grace, Harry and I were students together, he was like me. After what happened to him I have now become afraid. I feel my faith is not as strong as in the beginning, and for the first time in my life, I'm aware of how vulnerable I am.'

The Bishop looked hard at William and saw genuine fear in the eyes of a good man. It was times like this he wished he could pluck God from the Heavens and show his power was real. Walking around the desk, he stood beside and placed his hand on the young priests shoulder.

'Your faith is tired,' he said quietly, 'and though you are frightened, deep down you are really not disturbed. All this has come as a great shock to you but you will pass through it and carry on. Fr. Ferris is a priest who trifled with the grace of his vocation. That is a very dangerous thing to do. Anyone who does not rely on God alone is bound to fail. You have been given much, William, and much is expected of you.'

'But how can I know I won't betray Him?' asked William humbly.

'Even the Pope does not know that. All we can do is pray earnestly that we don't enter into temptation. Prayer, and knowing what we are, that is our only hope.'

'But I'm still ashamed of the anger that raged inside me.'

'Yes, that is understandable when you think of what those little boys must have been put through. But anger is an emotion to express how you feel. Jesus himself got angry when he whipped the traders out of the temple.'

'But I got so angry I could not hear Harry's confession and grant him forgiveness.'

'No you did not fail to hear him you only refused to listen, and considering your friendship and the circumstances, I think it was wrong of him to ask you in the first place.'

As the hours passed the two men talked and talked. For the first time in months William felt a great calmness come over his troubled mind. They were only interrupted once, and that was when the secretary came with some coffee and sandwiches.

He was surprised to find that despite the authority Bishop Commins held, underneath it all he was quite an understanding and compassionate man

As their meeting came to a close the Bishop further instructed William,

'Remember Jesus did not examine his cross.... he took it. He did not complain about the weight but summoned all his strength to carry it. He did not get so caught up in his own pain, that he could not see the sufferings of others. In times of trouble look to the cross, relive every moment of it. Then you might almost hear Him say;

'Forgive them for they do not know what they do.'

'I think I understand,' said William.

'Well, to hold on when hope and courage are at their lowest is hard even for the best of us. I think you come from genuine stock, William, and I know there are great things ahead of you.'

The Bishop then suggested a week's retreat at St. Anne's in Portarlington. There, William would find a quiet peace so necessary for prayer and reflection. William rose from his seat, and having kissed the Bishop's ring, turned for the door.

Picking up Mrs. Stapelton's letter the Bishop smiled as he called after him,

'Oh just a moment William, two last things.' he said lighter tone.

'Yes your Grace.'

'Will you eat your food and stop leaving the lights, you know none of us can afford to upset our housekeepers.'

Chapter 22.

It was over a week since Father William had returned from retreat and while away he had reflected on many things.

Having been worn down both physically and mentally over the last months, he found the peace of the retreat house a welcome refuge.

At first he found himself dwelling on all that had happened and his own life to date, but he soon grew weary of that as the same thoughts kept going round and round in his head. His prayers did not comfort him as they had lost their meaning and became just empty words.

He had been three days in the retreat house when one night, while sitting on his bed, he happened to glance up at a picture of the Virgin and Child hanging on the wall.

'Oh God,' he prayed desperately, 'I want you to take every prayer I have ever said and any good thing I have ever done and I want to lay them at your feet. Take them Lord and do something because I am lost.'

With that William got into bed and with a heavy heart he fell into an exhausted unhappy sleep.

The next morning he arose as usual. Remembering his prayer of the previous night, he felt no real change in the heavy darkness of his spirit. Looking out the window, he wondered how he would get through the dreary day ahead. After dressing, he was about to walk from the bedroom when his eyes fell on the picture again. Remembering his heartfelt prayer from the night before he gave a deep sigh. There seemed to be no change in him. He could still feel an awful heaviness in his spirit. Then, joining his hands, he stood once more before the picture and began praying.

He had just uttered the first words when a great feeling of joy entered his soul. Then, as he continued praying, he felt a great weight lift from his shoulders. Each word of his prayer became more heartfelt and meaningful, and for the first time, in a long while he felt he was communicating with a living person.

By the time he had finished, William had, with grateful tears, recaptured the joy he had lost. He began to think back to when he first got his vocation and how happy he was then. He thought back to his ordination and how that was even more wonderful. But put together, these times were nothing compared to the exultation he was now feeling.

His love for God now burned so intently in his heart and soul that he felt his human body might not be able to contain it. Feelings of relief, elation, peace and excitement surged through him, but at the same time it was Divine love alone that totally consumed him to the point of tears.

Having been lost in his own darkness for so long, William was now feeling the joy of God's love not just inside him but all around him. This was the moment William's faith came back and he would never forget it. Falling to his knees he bowed his head and said the most personal prayer of his life.

A little while later, as he was walking down the corridor towards the dining room, he decided not to tell anyone about his experience as he was afraid that in doing so he might lose the private and special wonder of it all.

Anyway they might not understand. Then as the day wore on, he hoped he would not revert back into the darkness. But that was not to be. Every time William prayed, his soul filled with even more fervour and his spirit drew closer in happiness and joy to the Lord.

During the following days he thought through everything Bishop Commins had said. He found that he had to agree with him that real grief, sorrow, and shame were private and that no two people could deal with them the same.

'Only God can fully understand the depth of another persons feelings,' the Bishop had explained, 'and that is why only God can forgive completely.'

However, through all his soul searching William slowly became aware of the power of sincere humility. He knew he would need to constantly demean himself if he were to reach the perfection of every other virtue. He took great comfort in knowing that with humility, he could face any suffering that might be in store for him and still remain faithful.

So with his faith reborn, stronger than ever, Fr. Thornton could now, in complete confidence, give God's blessing to his people at the end of morning Mass.

Afterwards, when everyone was gone, he remained on in the new church. Walking down the wide aisle and back up he looked knowingly at the Stations of the Cross hanging on both sides of the plain white walls.

Looking up at the marble altar, he remembered the care the people had taken when they removed it carefully from the old church and placed so reverently in the new one. Beams of colourful light from the exquisite stained glass window above the altar shone all around and added to the simple splendour of the sanctuary.

Kneeling down at the end of one of the new polished wooden seats, William felt good to know that the church was built by the people of Kilrowan as a splendid monument to God.

Then he grasped his hands tightly. Bowing his head in reverence, he repeated with love, the intimate prayer he had said with tears the night his faith returned to him:

Oh Lord I love you above all things,
You are in my thoughts and my being,
You reach in and touch my soul.
Gently you stroke my spirit until it no longer wants to dwell in human form but fly straight into your arms.
My God I love you.
My tears of regret reach out from my heart yet daily I fall from grace.
Oh Lord I cannot bear to be apart from you, look down on me now in my state of despair and use me as you see fit.
Oh most powerful God I bow before you and throw myself at your feet.
As much as I am insignificant you are powerful.
Forgive me Lord for not understanding that you are my life, my love, and my reason for living.
I have been in the dark without you and now I want to come back into your light. I denied you once but now I would gladly die for you.
Oh Lord My God I will never leave you again.'

A little while later William walked into the dining room in the Presbytery for his breakfast. Picking up 'The Irish Independent' newspaper, he unfolded it and sat down at the table. But before his eyes could take in the print, a large bold photograph stared back at him from the front page.

It was a horrible picture of Fr. Ferris. Having been taken from a very close angle, it emphasised and almost distorted the priest's worst features. Harold's usual bright eyes had taken on a staring look and seemed full of dark fear.

His slightly prominent teeth looked almost menacing. His thick hair stood out wildly from his head as if blown by a wind.

In the background of the photograph, William could just about see two Gardai. Then his eyes fell quickly to the caption below the photograph.

Words like monster, beast, and perverted priest jumped off the page at him. The more he read the more shocked he became. There in large black and white letters were the awful sufferings that Harold had inflicted on his victims. Each word struck like an arrow to William's heart and once more he felt a great repulsion.

While continuing to read he felt as if he himself stood accused. Then, as he finished moments later, it was as if all his fellow priests and the Catholic Church were being accused also.

'So you seen it have ya Father?' asked Mrs. Stapleton breaking into his thoughts as she brought his breakfast into the room.

'Isn't it dreadful,' she said, shaking her white head and placing his breakfast down in front of him on the table.

'Me stomach's sick I tell ya after readin' it. I was talkin' to Mrs. Brady after Mass and the poor woman is in shock too. It's the talk on everyone's lips. Where's it goin to end? Lord ya know, it would make ya ashamed to say ya were Catholic.'

William did not reply but rose quickly from his chair and went to look for Fr. Breen. He found the old priest in the office printing out Mass leaflets.

'Have you seen this Dan?' William asked urgently as he thrust the paper under Fr. Breen's nose.

'Yes I have read it,' said Fr Breen sadly,' Of course the media is busy as usual hyping up the situation.'

'But many people, our parishioners they are all upset by this,' said William.

'Of course they are and rightly so,' said Fr. Breen sympathetically.

'We have to do something, we've got to reassure them,' William said worriedly as he walked up and down the room.

Fr. Breen continued sorting the Mass leaflets.

'Until the media takes the heat off the situation we cannot begin to explain.'

'But the Church must speak out, we must defend the good priests, we cannot stay silent,' said William anxiously.

'No, you're wrong,' said Fr. Breen as he stopped what he was doing and looked up seriously at his curate.

'Just as Jesus remained calm and in control in the turmoil in Gethsamene, so the Church does with the media. She always reflects the spirit of Christ. She meets it with principles and compassion. She will not be forced to answer except in her own time. Her power lies in constructive dialogue based on truth from the gospels and also with suffering and endurance.'

After thinking for a moment William said,

'Yes, but the media is so powerful today, it stirs up people. They believe everything they read. It paints only the bad side and gives no help to the victims and their families. Evil is dwelled on so much that it shuts out any light on the case. So many have been hurt so deeply by this awful thing, surely we must be brave, we must speak out, we must do something.'

'No,' said Fr. Breen firmly looking up from under his glasses, 'In spiritual warfare natural courage and goodwill are only of some use. But we must rely on God alone to change each heart or we are sure to fail.'

William grew quiet. He understood what Fr. Breen was saying but still had a strong urge to go out and do something.

Folding the newspaper, he put it under his arm, turned and left the room.

Taking the stairs two steps at a time he rushed up to his bedroom. Closing the door tightly behind him he went over and sat down on the bed. Opening up the paper again he stared searchingly at Harold's picture.

Once again it was so hard to separate the man from the sin. How well William knew Harold's personality, but how little he knew of what lay behind those eyes. To know his very soul would have been impossible.

As William continued to stare at the photograph he once more thought back to their student days together, to the Harold before the perverseness.

He tried desperately to recall if there had been anything in the past that might have given him the slightest indication that his friend was capable of such a horrific crime. Having failed to do so he then started to think about the teaching on sexuality they received in Maynooth. It was true celibacy was discussed, yet he could not recall any of the professors telling them how to live with it and remain true to their normal feelings. He was also aware that sexuality had a great influence on some of the other priests lives.

He had felt sorry for the women and the priest's who had got involved down through the years, especially when he saw first hand the confusion and hurt it caused.

But William had fought hard to understand his own sexuality.

Left to him it would have been the most important thing in his life, but instead, he took his sexuality and went to the source of its Creator. There he found that by uniting it with all his other natural urges and to the purity of God, he was able to control them without suppression, to enjoy them without selfishness and to give thanks for the wisdom to know the difference. But by doing that he also prayed for the grace that he would be constantly compassionate to the people who were weak and gave in to their desires.

In the minutes that followed, William recalled the goodness that he saw in his friend many years ago. Suddenly he knew that no matter whether Harold was innocent or guilty he William, as a true Christian, was duty bound to help him and his family and see this thing to the end.

That evening Orla Stapleton walked out of the post office. Standing eye level with the post box she began checking the stamps.

Even with her usual efficiency, she failed to notice a particular name and address among the letters. Among the envelopes she was dropping into the box was a special one. A good friend was sincerely hoping to reach across the miles, and be of some help to an old one.

Chapter 23.

Life was never the same for Frank Furlong after the sudden and tragic death of his father and his aunt Hattie. For some strange reason, best known to himself, he did not want anyone else to take over the day- to- day running of the farm. So instead he decided to do it himself. But over the next few months the farm seemed to run a lot more smoothly than the housework. Now, just turned fifty, Frank's heavy thick black hair was starting to turn grey. Neighbours and friends remarked in amazement how he was becoming more like the Boss every day. Though not quite as tall as his father, he had a lot of his mannerisms and ways.

Of all days of the week it was Sunday that Frank dreaded the most. With the herding done, he would return to the cold house to cook his breakfast. He stubbornly followed his own strict regime. He did not bother to light the range, as he found the gas cooker much quicker.

He washed his cup, plate and utensils after every meal and then put them back at his place on the table.

After his good weekly scrub up, he would put on his best suit and drive to the village to attend eleven o' clock Mass. Not being one to gossip at the church gate or go to the pub, he usually went straight home after the service.

For the first few weeks after Walter died, David used to join him for Sunday lunch, but then for some strange reason he just stopped coming. But despite everything, Frank carried on the family tradition of cooking a roast on a Sunday. Opening the oven door, he would place freshly scrubbed potatoes in the sizzling juices. Then, closing it, he would smile as he inhaled the wonderful aroma. Once again it would bring back the comforts of the old days.

With his dinner cooking away, Frank would then take up the Sunday papers, sit down in the Boss's armchair and begin to read the week's events. All the previous Sunday papers were piled high on the stool beside him.

'I must burn some of them this week,' he thought to himself.

After dinner he would cover the rest of the tasty roast with tin foil and carefully put it in the fridge. This would be his meat for the next few days. Then, he would sit back into the armchair again and have a short snooze.

Having worked hard for six days, it was Sunday night he found the longest. Many an hour he sat with his ears straining to hear the sound of a car that might drive into the yard. It was during these times that he missed his family the most.

However, for the rest of the week the nights were not as lonely. He could be found ploughing, tilling or sowing until late. But because of the Furlong's faith nothing justified working on a Sunday.

It was while out ploughing, a couple of months later, on one such dark November night that Frank happened to see a red glow coming from the direction of 'Mount Benedict.'

Stopping the tractor, he opened the door, leaned out, and strained his eyes. On seeing a definite flicker in the glow he knew immediately what it meant. Turning the tractor around he drove quickly back to the yard and raced into the house. Reaching for the telephone he dialled some numbers with a shaking hand.

'Maureen, its Frank Furlong,' he said in a loud quick voice, 'your hay shed's on fire. Ring the fire brigade, I'm on my way over there.'

Within minutes he was in the jeep and driving at high speed towards the fire. Approaching the yard, he could see Lady Gowne and Charlie standing together looking up at the hay shed. It was one big red glowing mass of flames with bright sparks shooting up into the dark sky.

Suddenly his eyes were distracted by the sound of the horses as they whinnied and kicked frantically at the doors of the stables.

'Quick,' he said running in the direction of the stables, 'we've got to get the horses out.'

'No,' shouted Lady Gowne frantically as she went to stop him, 'We've tried but it's too dangerous. The electricity gone and...' before she could finish Frank pulled his top coat over his head and ran into the darkness.

On reaching the stables he quickly unbolted each of the doors. As the frightened horses emerged from the thick black smoke, Lady Gowne and Charlie tried to shoo them into the open paddock. When they were all safely there they closed the gate and, turning, they strained their eyes in an effort to see Frank. By now some of the sheets of galvanize had come loose from the shed and were crashing noisily on the concrete yard. This terrible sound frightened Lady Gowne even more. Feeling really worried, about Frank she began to shout out his name. As the minutes went by there was still no sign and they began to fear the worst. Drawing back from the intense heat, they continued calling out frantically. Then all other sounds gave way to the urgent blaring of the fire brigades as they screamed along the road and under the large beech trees approaching the yard. The firemen quickly took control of the situation immediately and told everybody to stand well back. Lady Gowne continued to call out frantically for her neighbour. Eventually she saw a lone figure stumbling from the darkness of the field. A feeling of tremendous relief rushed through her as she hurried to help him. Coughing and gasping Frank tried desperately to catch his breath.

'Did the horses get out alright?' he asked breathlessly. 'Yes,' she said thankfully, 'But that was very foolish what you just did you could have been killed.'

'No, I'm alright,' he said, still choking a little.

Lady Gowne put her arm around his shoulder. 'Lets get you inside there's nothing more we can do now.'

The warmth of the Aga cooker was very comforting when they walked into the kitchen. In the beam of their flash lamps Lady Gowne put the kettle on to boil.

'Charlie will you get Frank a glass of water, I'm going to answer that wretched phone.' she said as she went into the hall.

A few moments later she returned.

'That was Major Fennel,' she said rather annoyed, 'he's heard about the fire and he is coming over. I told him there's nothing he can do now, but the damn fellow insists,' she said looking distressed.

Charlie poured out a cup of tea and handed it to her. She clasped the hot cup gratefully between her trembling cold hands. Looking as if she was about to cry, Frank stood up and said thoughtfully:

'Are you alright?'

'Oh yes, I'm just a little shaken.'

By now the neighbours had started to arrive, some of them wanted to help while others just came to look.

'Charlie, let's get out there and stop them coming in at the gate. Tell them we're okay and that the fire brigade has everything under control,' she said sternly. Following behind him she stood in the yard with her coat wrapped tightly around her.

Almost in a daze, she watched the firemen hosing down what was left of her indoor stables.

'Oh thank God it's not going to spread any further,' she said looking up at the smouldering shed.

It was seven a.m. before the firemen were satisfied that their work was completed. Lady Gowne thanked them gratefully. Charlie collected their empty mugs and they began packing up their gear. After they had left Frank walked with Lady Gowne over to the twisted black metal that used to be the hay shed.

As they stood in silence looking at it, Frank felt so sorry for her. Walking over, he put his hand comfortingly on her shoulder.

With that she burst out crying and put her two arms around his shoulders. As her body trembled in his arms Frank stood firm and fought back his own tears. He knew the heartbreak she was going through. Eventually she looked up at him and said:

'How can I thank you for all you've done for me.'

'I've done nothin',' he said awkwardly.

'Oh but you did,' she insisted, 'you saved my horses.'

'But what are ya goin' to do now?'

'I don't honestly know, I just can't think.'

'I'll tell ya what, Doireann's stables are still vacant up at my place, you're welcome to use them if you need to.'

Suddenly she remembered the night Doireann saved Propeller and she broke out into a slight hysterical laugh.

'Goodness,' she said, letting out a deep sigh, 'I don't know what I would do without you Furlongs, it seems every time I have a crisis one of you comes to my aid.'

Suddenly a loud voice broke the moment.

'Damn bad luck Maureen what.'

When they turned they saw Major Fennel marching towards them.

Frank quickly stepped to one side and shoved his hands in his pocket.

With his face a little redder than usual, the Major quickly put his arm around Lady Gowne and said:

'Don't worry about a thing my dear lady, I have it all worked out. I shall make some of my stables available to you for your horses immediately and …'

As he continued speaking, Frank looked over at his rather agitated neighbour and smiled:

'I'll leave yez to it,' he whispered and slipped quietly away.

It was 9 o' clock in the morning when he eventually returned home. Feeling very tired from being up all night, he walked slowly into the kitchen and stood quite still. For the first time in his life he noticed that there was complete and total silence in the big house.

There was not even the sound of the clock ticking.

With his body exhausted and feeling stiff and his mind racing, he grew restless and wandered out into the hall. Opening the large front door, he sat down wearily on the end step of the stairs. Then he stared thoughtfully up into the morning sky. Having not admitted to Lady Gowne just how near he had come to choking to death, he began to wonder what would have happened if he had died in the fire. His love and dedication to the animals almost cost him is life just as it had with the Boss.

Then he remembered how good it felt just to hold another human being in his arms. Jumping to his feet, he walked over to the door and leaned against the frame. Looking out across the bleakness of the fields he thought sadly:

'Maybe, I've missed out on the real happiness that life has to offer.'

Then, turning around, he looked up the stairs. With the loneliness of the house once more creeping into his bones he banged his fist on the door and shouted:

'Damn it, there's only one person who can do something about this, and that's me.'

Whipping his cap off the hallstand, he then changed his mind and threw it back again. Then pulling the hall door heavily behind him, he hurriedly went outside. At last he was admitting to himself that he needed more than the land could ever give him.

Walking with big strides across the long meadow, he was now going to do what he should have done all those years ago. Frank Furlong was determined to make up for the biggest mistake of his life.

Chapter 24.

Biddy Brown walked out of Kenny's Grocery Store with her two heavy plastic bags stuffed to capacity. Lifting them up, she just about managed to wrap the plastic handles around the bars of her bike. Then, with her little son sitting patiently on the carrier she lifted her leg onto the pedal and cycled off down the road. Two of the women from the village watched as she rode by.

'That's a strange one you know, keeps to herself a lot.'

'Hmm, pity she didn't do that before Frank Furlong made an eejit out of her.'

'Yeah, but you know, it serves them right, those Brown's, they always thought they were better than the rest of us, and I wouldn't mind only her mother was an alcoholic.'

'Aye she was too.'

'Ould Furlong wasn't long getting' shut of her when he found out there was a baby on the way.'

'No and sur, wasn't he right.'

Then as they watched Biddy disappear from their sight the older one said curiously:

'But wouldn't ya wonder what she does all day.'

When Biddy arrived back home she lifted her son down off the bike and opened the door. Completely engrossed in his new toy, the boy went inside and sat down on the couch. Then, as she struggled with the shopping bags, both of them were unaware that the peace of the morning was about to be broken. Suddenly the kitchen door opened and Frank Furlong walked in as awkwardly as ever. Biddy almost dropped the jars in her hand. The little boy jumped up and ran quickly behind his mother.

'Frank, what are ya doin' here, is there somethin' wrong?' she asked worriedly as she noticed his distressed state.

Suddenly remembering the dirt of his clothes Frank informed her of the fire of the previous night.

'I thought I heard the fire engine, was there anyone hurt.'

'No, but the indoor stables were destroyed.'

'Are you alright?' she asked concernedly.

With a great dazed look on his face he slowly replied:

'No... yes... damn it Biddy, everythin' is wrong, it's all my fault.
'The fire...?'
'No, I don't mean that, I mean... I've been a total eejit'
'How?'
'I mean about us.'

At these words Biddy looked back at the little boy. Having reassured him that everything was alright, she then told him to go to his room and play. Closing the door behind him, she quickly walked over to her unexpected visitor and whispered:

'Us?'

Frank looked at her in a most childlike way,

'I'm not makin' much of a job of this am I? '

'No yer not,' she said angrily as she walked over and closed the door behind him.

'Ya just barge in here talkin' about us. But there is no us.'

Frank pulled out a chair at the end of the table and sat down. Running his fingers through his smoky windswept hair he began,

'Look Biddy, what I'm tryin' to say is I'm sorry I didn't stick by ya and stand up to the Boss. I let ya go through havin' the baby on yer own, I could stay here all evenin' sayin' I'm sorry, I can't believe I was so stupid.'

Reaching his hand out to her he said sincerely:

'Ya see Biddy, for the first time in me life I realize what it's like to be lonely. Then it dawned on me what you must have gone through in the last few years. I want to make it up to ya Biddy.'

Suddenly all the hurt and rejection she had suffered welled up inside her. Holding her chin up proudly, she sat down at the other end of the table and said in a cold voice:

'The Boss, God rest him, took care of everythin' we don't want for nothin.'

'Damn it Biddy I've not come here to talk about money, I've come about feelins'...your feelins,...my feelins.'

Suddenly seeing a side to Frank she never saw before Biddy asked curiously: 'So what is it you're tryin to say?'

He shuffled awkwardly in his seat. Wanting to hold her hand, he restrained himself, and instead looked across with all the sincerity he could muster.

'Biddy will ya marry me?'

As her eyes opened wide in surprise she immediately stood up and started walking nervously around the kitchen.

With her heart beating a little faster now she thought to herself:

'Why didn't he ask me before, when I really wanted him to.'

Then out loud she said angrily:

'Frank Furlong, ya have some cheek. Ya think ya can come in here, after all this time, and expect me to marry ya just like that, just because yer lonely and fed up on yer own.'

Finding it hard to remain in his seat, Frank protested,

'No that's not it, I really want to marry ya.'

'But why do ya want to marry me now?'

He suddenly blushed deeply and said awkwardly

'Because I know I love ya and I always have.'

A silence descended on the room. Wanting to believe him, but still not trusting his words, she quickly covered up her true feelings.

'Well ya have a funny way of showin' it, ya leave me here without even comin' to see yer own son, now out a the blue ya tell me this.'

Frank got up from his seat and braced himself. He was ready to take all her angry accusations like a man.'

'But what about me? ya didn't ask if I still love ya,' she shouted at him, 'Ya've asked me nothin, ya think I'd here waitin for ya. For all ya know I could have found someone else.'

Quickly glancing around the kitchen he asked worriedly:

'And have ya?'

'No,' she said smugly as she turned towards the window, 'but I could have.'

Walking over beside her he gently took her hand.

' Biddy lets stop playin' games with one another. Remember how we were in the past? Ya know how well we got on together, you're like me, ya have a wild passion about ya and I've always loved ya for it.'

Thinking back to the fun they had together, she began to soften a little, but old hurt feelings still came to the surface.

'Yeah, well, when ya didn't stand up to the Boss that time and let me be treated like dirt, now that hurt, it really hurt."

Then, turning to face him with her eyes flashing, she said in a serious voice:

'That's the kind of thing that kills love.'

Frank's eyes suddenly took on a frightened expression and in that moment Biddy knew she still had her power over him.

Just then the bedroom door opened gently and the little boy, completely engrossed in the new toy that his mother bought him earlier, wandered unnoticed into the kitchen.

'Okay,' said Biddy, calming down a little,' Ya say ya want ta marry me. Ya does it matter to ya whether I love ya or not?'

'But ya do don't ya Biddy?' he asked hopefully.

'Do I what?' she asked teasingly.

Moving his body a little closer to her, he asked again:

'Do ya still love me?'

Ignoring his question Biddy suddenly caught sight of their son.

'What about the boy?'

'I've been through hell and high water over the last five years. Not a day went by that I didn't think of him,' he whispered back.'

Doubting his words Biddy looked up to heaven.

'So tell me, when was he born?' she asked impatiently.

Without hesitation Frank was able to give her the time, the date and to her surprise, even his weight.

Opening her eyes in wide amazement, she asked curiously:

'How di ya know all that?'

'Cos I rang the hospital to see if everythin' was all right.'

'Well if ya were so concerned where were ya on his birthdays?'

Looking over at his son, Frank said quietly,

'I was too ashamed and anyway I thought ya must hate me.'

'Ashamed ya mean you were a coward.'

'I don't blame ya for thinkin' that Biddy, I've hurt ya and let ya down, but that's in the past.'

Then, taking her face in his hands, he said:

'And in spite of everythin' that happened I think ya still love me.'

'You mean you'd like to think I still love ya,' she said with a devilment in her eye.

'I repeat my question, what about yer son?'

'Well, I'd sure as hell like the chance to get to know him,' said Frank, winking over at the boy.

'And what kind of a father do ya think ya'd make?'

'Probably a lousy one,' he said, shrugging his shoulders.

'Look Frank, this isn't funny, I need ta know before I answer yer question of marriage.'

Putting his hands on her shoulders, he said with a desperate panic in his voice:

'Biddy if ya just give me the chance I swear I'll spend the rest of my life makin' it up to you. I'll ask ya one more time. Will ya marry me?'

'Sorry, I didn't hear ya,' she said seriously as she held her ear lobe.

Raising his voice he said very slowly:

'Will...ya...marry...me?'

'Yes I will.'

With that, a big broad smile spread across his face as he swept her up into his strong arms. As Biddy hugged him she looked down at the little boy laughing on the couch. Then, a sudden thought came to her that banished all the lonely years of pain and humiliation.

'Yeah I'll marry ya alright,' she thought happily, 'and my son will be Master of 'Riversdale House.'

Chapter 25.

A small crowd of local people watched with sadness as the old wooden sign 'J.J. Malone Fish Shop' was lowered to the ground, and a flashy neon one saying 'Coombe Electrical' raised up and put in its place. When the workmen left, some of the onlookers went over and inspected the neglected sign more closely. As memories of the old days came flooding back, one woman bent down, touched it gently and walked away sadly, shaking her head as she went.

Inside the shop the white walls and modern fittings brought a different feel to the place. Over the past few weeks David had a few misgivings as they took the old blue tiles up off the shop floor. But it was while removing the big wooden counter, the scales and the fish barrels, the old memories came back to haunt him.

The horse and cart boys, however, did not share in his nostalgia as they handed over their money and drove happily away with their purchases. These old fittings would fetch a good price with the antique dealers on Francis Street. Having turned what was formally his and Molly's first home, up over the shop, into a store,

David was careful to put their bed into what had been McDermott's house next door.

Now as the day of opening their shop for the first time had dawned, David and Matty smiled proudly at each other. All their hard work had paid off. Dressed in new brown shop coats, in total contrast to the soiled aprons that J.J. and Molly used to wear, they proceeded to show curious customers the latest washing machines, cookers, electric fires, etc on the market.

But despite the excitement and optimism of being happy with what they had achieved, deep down David knew that something more important to him was missing. Alishe his wife had promised to call to the shop after work, but as the evening wore on there was still no sign of her.

Then, after closing time, he left a note pinned to the door, saying she could find him in the Fleury's pub down the street. But, after the one celebratory pint with Matty, he looked at his watch and decided it was time to head home.

As he drove back to Bray he sighed deeply. He was so tired of the cat and mouse games that she was playing lately. He knew she had been upset in the beginning that he had not sold the premises, but he still expected her to turn up for the opening.

On arriving at their apartment, he was just turning the key in the lock when anxiously she opened the door.

'Oh I'm glad you're here darling I'm having a small party. Now hurry up and get changed, I collected your suit from the cleaners and it's laid out on the bed.'

Thinking the party was to celebrate the opening of his shop David smiled happily and hurried upstairs.

'She really does care,' he thought to himself.

Once again he decided to forgive her for her noticeable absence as she had obviously gone to a lot of bother with this party. He wondered if Matty had known about it, and if he did he was certainly good at keeping a secret.

As he showered and dressed he whistled happily. With the tension and hard work of the previous weeks over, he now had quite an appetite. However, when he walked down the stairs a little later, and saw all the unfamiliar faces in his living room he looked over at Alishe in dismay.

'David darling, come and meet my friends,' she said, smiling.

Looking around, it slowly dawned on him that this party was not to celebrate his new business venture at all. It was exclusive to her so called elite circle of friends. Feeling angry, his silk tie suddenly seemed to be choking him, so loosening it, and opened the top button of his blue shirt. Then he went over to the small table and poured himself out a stiff drink. Being equally as educated and cultured as his wife's guests, he found he had no time for their false conversation and their hollow laughter. Standing at the drink's table, he held and twisted the crystal glass slowly in his hand. Alishe looked over and crossly signalled to him to straighten his tie. Then she introduced some of the new faces that had invaded their home.

Just then one of her colleagues, puffing great clouds of smoke from his cigar, reached over and shook David's hand.

'Your lovely wife has been telling us all about your new venture in the electrical trade old boy. Must say we wish you well. Now your choice of location would not be the best however, I believe a lot of thieving goes on around there.'

Suddenly, something began to boil up inside David. The Coombe might be one of the poorer areas of Dublin, but the majority of the people living there were the salt of the earth.

'I find that very interesting,' replied David angrily, 'especially as my late wife and my in-laws came from there.'

Coughing loudly, the older man turned embarrassingly to his companion and quickly changed the subject. Relieving the tension of the moment, Alishe asked everyone to join her in the dining room.

Looking down at the cold buffet of seafood and salad on the large table, instead of a nice hot meal, David grew more disappointed.

Then, when he was about to try some of the unusual culinary delights, an obnoxious little bore came up and stood beside him, his large gold wristwatch and strong after shave annoying him further. As he tried to listen to the silly man, he watched Alishe going around encouraging her guests to help themselves. Suddenly his heart felt sickened and the food began to stick in his throat.

Finding it hard to relax, he put down his plate, left the room and went into the kitchen. Seeing this, Alishe excused herself and followed him.

'What is the matter with you tonight?' she said angrily under her breath, 'Why are you acting like this?'

Leaning against the counter, he just looked blankly at her.

'Well, if you won't speak to me I'm going back inside.'

Turning on her heel, she quickly walked out the door.

After she had gone David stood alone. Listening to the conversation in the next room, it was only now he was beginning to realise that Alishe had outgrown him. She had no interest in his business, his daughter or his hopes for their future.

These people and her career were all that was important to her now. He thought back to when they first met and how different it all was then. In the beginning he really believed he could combine the two lives, working on the farm all week and coming to the city at the weekends. But over the years they had slowly grown apart. He knew it was not all her fault. Still tonight he felt there was no point in discussing it any more. It would only lead to another row and God knows they had had enough of them.

Suddenly he had a great urge to get away. Walking back out through the dining room, he moved quickly and excused himself between her guests.

On reaching the bedroom he took down a large suitcase from on top of the wardrobe. Then, opening the drawers of the mahogany tallboy, he began packing. Within minutes the door opened and Alishe, with eyes flashing, walked into the room.

'David I'm so angry with you, you are once again behaving like a spoilt child.'

Not wanting to get into anther useless argument, David stopped packing, straightened up and in a loud voice shouted:

'Shut up Alishe, I've got something to tell you.'

Looking gobsmaked at her husband's rudeness, for once she was dumbfounded.

'I want out now,' he demanded.

'Out of what?' she asked, puzzled.

'Out of this house and this bloody marriage,' he said angrily as he brushed past her and opened the door of the wardrobe.

Her cold eyes flashed with temper.

'You want it, just like that,' she said, clicking her long fingers.

Waving his hand determinedly, he past in front of her and continued packing.

'I'm not going to argue about this my mind's already made up. Everything I have ever felt for you is gone, and to be honest, I don't think you are capable of loving anyone but your self.'

'Hold on now David, it's not as simple as that,' she said, looking around their luxurious bedroom, 'What about all this?'

Closing the lid on his suitcase, he lifted it off the bed. 'You're the solicitor sort it out,' he said as he made for the door.

Then she sat down on their bed as angry tears suddenly welled up in her eyes. Looking down at her wedding ring, for a split second she thought to go after him. Then she heard a loud burst of laughter from the party below. Lifting her proud head she stood up and straightened her dress.

'Yes, I am the solicitor, David Furlong,' she said in defiance, 'and I'm a bloody good one, it would do you well to remember that.'

Meanwhile David, accompanied by the sound of the same laughter, hurried down the stairs. Unaware of their host's dramatic departure the guests continued to enjoy themselves.

As he reached the front door David looked back one more time, hoping for what, he did not know. But as he pulled the heavy hall door behind him he did not hear a sound.

After closing the boot of the car he looked up sadly at the warm glow in the window of the front room. Then he sat into the car and drove to the only place he felt was his home. Turning the corner into the street, he pulled up at his shop. Switching off the engine he leaned wearily on the steering wheel.

Then, in the great quiet loneliness that came over him, he thought he heard a ghostly whisper.

Raising his head, he looked around as he suddenly heard it again.

This time he knew who it was. Tears welled up in his eyes as he thought he heard from the past his only darling say:

'Oh David nobody will ever love you like I do.'

Chapter 26.

As Father Thornton sat on a south- bound train he buried his head in his hands. Shaking his weary head with sheer bewilderment, he thought of the many things that had happened in the last few days. Frank's surprise phone call when he rang to ask his help to marry Biddy and adopt their child, David's sad news about the break up of his marriage, and not least the very disturbing letter that had arrived the same morning from Liverpool. Reaching into his pocket, he pulled out the letter. Reading it again, he still felt hurt that Molly had gone and secretly married Edgar Archer in a registry office in England.

Further stern words from Father Breen that he may be neglecting his parish only added to his troubles as he thought of the difficult task that lay ahead of him. From the moment he got Harold's letter a week ago now, he found he could think about nothing else. He had learned that while awaiting trial Harold was out on his own bail.

William wondered how Harold felt now that he had been charged. He was relieved that his friend had admitted his guilt, and that his superiors, who previously not wanting to bring scandal down on the church, had not as usual hushed it up, or, worse still, transferred him to another diocese. This time William hoped he would have the courage and wisdom to face the situation and be able to help. Then as the train pulled into the station, he bowed his head and in a humble silence asked God to help him.

Alighting with the other passengers on to the platform, he looked up and down to see if he could recognise Harold among the people. But instead he could only see Harold's father, Mr. Ferris. A small thin man in his late sixties, he removed his peaked cap when he saw William, and his thin wispy grey hair blew untidily in the wind.

Looking up gratefully into William's friendly eyes, Mr. Ferris held out a thin cold blue-red hand and shook William's hand vigorously.

'Thanks for comin' father,' he said sincerely,' you'll never know just how much it means to us.'

William asked concernedly: 'How is Harry? Is he here?'

'No, he's gone for a walk,' replied Mr. Ferris sadly.

'He's doin' that a lot lately and I don't expect him back until later.' Then sadly he whispered, 'He's gone quiet in himself, gone very quiet.'

Then he turned around to lead the way towards his car.

As they drove along the bumpy country roads the old man talked on and on about his family. It was as if he was searching back through the generations to find out what went wrong.

He told William how Harold was the first religious in the family. He spoke about how proud his wife was of him and how everyone had said that a priest in the family was a great blessing.

At one stage William, on hearing the emotion in his voice, thought that the old man was going to cry. Then he began telling of the sacrifices they had made down through the years, to support Harold in the seminary. All their neighbours and friends held them in great respect for it. Now their friends could be counted on one hand.

William reached across the seat and put his hand supportively on the old man's shoulder. It was then it began to dawn on him that

Harold's family were now having to bear the heavy burden of Harold's sin.

'I don't know what to make of herself Father', he continued sadly, 'she just sits in the house and is too ashamed to leave it.'

As they turned off the main road into a narrower one and up a short avenue, William saw a two-storied old house looming in the distance.

The curtain moved slightly in a downstairs window as they dove up and around the back.

'We have to go in this way, the front door sticks in the cold weather,' explained Mr. Ferris as he switched off the engine.

'Oh and I'm sorry but ye may mind yer shoes with the muck.'

William watched his steps across the yard then smiled when he saw the line-up of rubber boots against the wall.

'This could be any house in my parish,' he thought happily.

When they walked into the large kitchen, a small petite woman with sharp features rose quickly from her chair

With her short grey hair held neatly at either side by combs, she looked at Father William with a lovely softness in her eyes. Then, with a half run, she rushed over to him and reached out with trembling hands.

Suddenly she burst into uncontrollable sobbing and clutched his sleeve tightly. Her thin lips began to quiver, and in a moment the softness in her eyes had changed to a desperate fear.

Embarrassed and a little shocked, her husband tried to pull her away but William looked understandingly at him and shook his head.

As he held her trembling body against his chest he thought back to the day of his ordination. That was the first time he had met this lovely couple. He regretted now that he had lost touch over the years and did not get to know them better.

Walking with Mrs. Ferris back to the chair she had risen from, William sat her down gently. Eventually she stopped sobbing and spoke to him.

'Oh Father,' she said sadly, 'I'm so ashamed but I love my son.'

'I know exactly how you feel, but you have done your duty,' said William as he stooped down beside her.

'Ah but you don't understand my heart is sore. It's as if it's being pulled from my chest and torn in two. This house has become a prison, I fear to answer the door or lift the phone. I have not able to bear reading the papers and some of the awful letters that we have received. I understand the hurt these people have suffered. But it would have been easier to bury my son than to have to go through this, this is a dreadful thing"

'Again I say, you have both done your duty,' said William, letting go of her hand, 'but somehow I think that the worst is over. Harry has faced up to his actions. We know now that he needs help, and whatever happens he may come out of this a better person. Remember, Mrs. Ferris Jesus said, that He came not for the righteous but for sinners.'

Thinking for a few moments, Mrs. Ferris asked worriedly:

'Will the church take any action against him, will they defrock him?'

'I really could not say, every case is different.'

'Maybe,' she went on, 'when all this has died down they might send him out on the missions.'

'To be quite honest I don't think so,' replied William seriously, 'What he has done is a very serious offence. I think he will have to serve some time in prison.'

'Oh no Father,' said Mrs. Ferris and she started to cry again.

Looking over at her husband with a tired pale face she began to shake as she said loudly:

'Did ya hear that Robbie? Father says they will be sending Harry to prison.'

Mr. Ferris took his cap off and looked over at William.

'Is this true?'

'Well I don't really know, I just said it could be a possibility.'

'I thought you came here to help,' said Mr. Ferris under his breath as he started to wash his hands.

Sensing a delicate situation about to go wrong William pulled out another chair and said quietly:

'Why don't we all sit down while we have the kitchen to ourselves. There are a few things I would like to say to you.'

Her husband dried his hands, picked up the kettle from the range and made three quick cups of tea.

As William sat in the warmth of the large kitchen he noticed the Sacred Heart picture hanging over the cooker. On opposite walls hung pictures of Harold's ordination. One was of him blessing his parents and the other was with the newly ordained priest with the rest of the family. The room was full of bright ornaments and colourful crockery, but in some corners, like beside the dresser and up over the clock, it was beginning to show signs of neglect.

The mug of tea when it came was most welcome.

As soon as they were all settled at the table William took a deep breath and began.

'What Harry has done is a very serious crime and I'm not going to try to gloss over it. He has actually sexually abused six boys. He has admitted his crime and he is going to plead guilty at the trial. This means that the boys may not have to give evidence. From then on he will be at the mercy of the court and his sentence will depend on the judge on the day.'

A silence came over the kitchen as both Harold's parents bowed their heads in shame. Mr. Ferris began rubbing the outside of his mug with his thumb. Slowly, and without looking up, he said in a low voice:

'I ask meself a thousand times a day how could my son do this? I did me best for him.'

'God knows that you both did your duty as parents,' said William sympathetically, 'we're only human and even in the best of situations things can go wrong. I've thought about this so much in the last couple of weeks and one explanation came to my mind. But that is all it is mind you an explanation, in no way is it an excuse. Harry left this family at the young age of thirteen to go to the seminary didn't he?'

'Well yes,' replied Mr. Ferris, suddenly thinking back, 'but if I remember he was really looking forward to going.'

'Yes,' continued William, 'But he missed out on his puberty and mixing with girls. Like us all, his sexuality was important, even sacred to him, but it was never allowed to develop. In fact you could say his sexuality was mentally abused. Then in the seminary it was further suppressed and hardly discussed. Then, years later, when Harry was ordained and went out into society he could only relate sexually to where he was taken from and that unfortunately was with children.'

Mr. Ferris thought for a moment and then said:

'That maybe, but it was a bad thing what he did.'

'Well,' said William, shaking his head,' the devil is as intelligent as he is evil. He is constantly watching us and especially priests. When he finds any weakness he quickly gets his foot in, so to speak. No one ever has peace who is a slave to passion.'

'But,' argued Mrs. Ferris, 'surely when Harry came back into society the good priests and people would have helped him stay on the right road?'

'No, Mrs. Ferris,' said William, as the smell of the sweet fresh bread seeped from the oven, 'each person is created to save his own soul. From being so long in a place of strict rules and spirituality, Harry was then suddenly thrown back into the world. Today it abounds with pornography and sensuality. It has seeped into our grocery shops, the internet, the television and even the mobile phones, its all around us. It is hard to escape it and some people drink it in like water. But you see its not until somebody gets hurt, and I mean someone very close to us, that we suddenly realise the terrible consequence of this evil. Then we put all the blame on the criminal.'

'Oh no,' said Mrs. Ferris getting upset and jumping up from the table, 'that's what my son is now, a criminal. I can never hold me head up again,' and she began crying into her apron.

Taking her hand, William looked into her tear-filled eyes.

'Come now,' he said gently, 'let me give you a name. Let me say the name... Mary. See her walk in a street full of people. These people are spitting and shouting at Her and Her Son.

They're so angry, so full of hate that they're ready to tear the clothes from His back and crucify Him. She stands helplessly watching while they humiliate mock and torture her son, and Her Son is guilty of no crime. Do you think she was worried about what the neighbours would say? Do you think She was worried about the disgrace to the family?

How do you think She got through that?'

The old woman looked down at William with tear filled eyes.

'I suppose she was praying,' she said quietly.

'Yes,' said William hitting the table, 'that's exactly what she was doing.'

Then he let go of her hand and spoke directly to the two of them. As he spoke his face took on the light of holiness.

'The evil that has descended on your home will either make it a prison or try to drive you out. The small things you loved and took pleasure in before this happened will suddenly become meaningless and distasteful. The illusion of anything worthwhile will seem to be outside of this place. You will begin to neglect the people you love and the way of life you once valued. This in turn will make your hearts grow very cold and drive out any peace that you have.

But I'm telling you now cling to your home. Shut out evil like you would a mad dog at your back door. Make your home a holy sanctuary from the troubles of the world. Remember the love you shared and the dreams you dreamed within theses four walls. You have to face up to what Harry has done and then you have to find the courage to forgive him for it. Otherwise it will destroy the rest of your life. Then you must pray like you've never prayed before. Don't just use words to implore God's help, but get down on your knees and pray with your very tears. Storm heaven if that's what it takes to get your peaceful loving home back.'

The two old people were visibly moved by the sheer confidence of what William said. Mrs. Ferris suddenly saw light in what seemed to be a very dark tunnel. Immediately her spirit lifted. Kneeling down quickly on the floor, she asked William if he would pray with them.

As the two men joined her there was really only one prayer William knew in his heart he could say. That prayer was by a man who had lived in suffering and died in obedience. It was the beautiful prayer of Saint Francis.

'Lord make me an instrument of your peace.
Where there is hatred let me sow love,
Where there is injury, pardon.
Where there is doubt, faith.
Where there is despair, hope
Where there is darkness, light and where there is sadness, joy.
Oh Divine Master, grant that I may not so much seek to be consoled as to console,
To be understood as to understand, to be loved as to love.
For it is giving that we receive,
It is in pardoning that we are pardoned,
It is in dying to ourselves, that we are born to eternal life.'

Chapter 27.

A couple of weeks later Father William opened the door of his car and sat into the driver's seat. Then, after shutting it, he put both hands on the steering wheel and leaned forward. His body shook as he breathed a great sigh of relief.

In the last few hours he had managed to visit six families and lay himself down as a living apology and mediator between Harold's victims and the Church. Having come up against rejection by three of the families, he was admitted by two, and really only welcomed by one. He worried now about their children, as he feared they might never get help.

Every emotion possible had been drawn from him as he went among them. It was only now, back in the enclosed privacy of his car, that he could at last breathe a sigh of relief.

It was a month ago since Fr. Ferris had been sentenced to eight years in prison. Father William had stayed with the family right through the trial. It was hard to watch his friend, who once had so much respect as a priest, sit with head bowed shamefully in the dock remaining silent. There were a few times during those terrible days when William thought Harold's parents would break down. The whole ordeal weighed heavy on their shoulders and caused them untold sorrow.

Then, at the end of those terrible days, as Harold was being led away, to begin his sentence, he suddenly looked back. William was standing beside Harold's mother and was not sure at which of them the look was intended. But one thing was sure it would be a long time before he would forget it. Harold's blank dark eyes stared out through his pale face as though from a bottomless pit.

It was in the silence of the journey back to the farmhouse that William began thinking about the whole thing. With the newspapers reporting on the trial, he took very much to heart the sufferings of all of the young victims.

Despite what Fr. Breen had said before about remaining silent, William knew that he would not rest until he had at least offered some help to the families involved.

Now, a month later, as he looked out of the car window, his mind went back over the last hours he had spent with them.

It had been a lovely autumn afternoon with the bright sunshine keeping the chill of the fresh wind at bay. He had decided to park his car at the entrance to the housing estate and walk instead. As he got out of the car he was well aware that he could be heading towards real anger, resentment and even understandable hatred. He had thought earlier of casting off his clerical clothes for more casual ones, but then decided against it.

If he was to represent Christ and his Church then he must not be ashamed of his attire, even if they might arouse resentment and anger. After locking his car, he straightened his jacket and took the first steps.

Taking a piece of paper from his pocket he checked over the names of the victims and their families. Having done a little research earlier, William did not need to inquire as to where they lived. The two-storied cement houses stretched before him in neat rows.

As he walked on, he could see curtains and shadows moving in the downstairs windows. Housewives chatting to each other across low walls suddenly grew quiet as he passed by. Some children ran on ahead as if to warn others of his coming.

As he approached the first house a small thin obnoxious women shouted at him from across the way:

'We've no children for ya today Father ya may go look elsewhere.'

Then her voice broke out into a loud mocking evil laugh. The horrible sound seemed to echo off the surrounding walls. William stopped for a moment but then he walked on and up a short path to a chipped dirty brown door. Hesitating a little, he then pressed the bell. Within minutes the door opened and William was facing a large red - faced woman dressed in a navy crossover apron.

Behind her and sitting halfway up on the stairs was a small frightened boy of about ten.

'Good afternoon,' said William politely, but before he uttered another word the woman leaned forward and spat hatefully into his face. Then she closed the door with an unmerciful bang. William took his handkerchief from his pocket and wiped the spittle away.

Then he rang the bell again. He rang four more times but the door remained firmly shut so William turned sadly away.

As he walked on he was now conscious of people watching his every move. The next house was down a good bit from the first and around a corner.

On ringing the doorbell, a tall thin woman with a cigarette dangling from her crooked lips opened the door. After explaining why he had come she welcomed William inside. Then between coughs, she looked up the stairs and shouted for her son to come down. Within minutes a hardy boy of thirteen bounded noisily down the stairs.

However, as mother and son talked to William he sensed a cold aggressiveness in their attitude. But he was unprepared when she asked quite casually:

'Maybe you could tell us where to go to get compensation Father?'

Completely taken aback, William tried to explain that that was not what he had come about. But they would not hear of anything else, so he was quickly shown the door.

Walking back to his car the autumn sun seemed to have given up on the day and hid shyly behind the thick black clouds gathering overhead. Looking up at the sky, William began hoping that he would make it back to the car before it rained.

Turning the car around a little while later, he left the estate and headed out on the country road. The next house was three miles away and he drove slowly around some dangerous wet corners.

When he arrived at the third house he saw a small lady watering her plants in the front porch. When she saw William's car pulling up she opened a white shining aluminium door. Steeping out he introduced himself, and as he talked to her he noticed her worried eyes looking up and down the road.

When he had finished speaking she whispered in a low voice:

'Ah you're very good Father to come here. Sur, it was a shockin' thing to happen. Now I'm afraid I can't let ya in cos I'd have to ask me husband. Ya see he's not like me, I love the Church and I realize yer all not to blame for this, but me husband is different. He never liked the Church and when this happened it really finished him with anything Catholic, do ya know what I mean. But I'll tell ya what I'll do, I'll ask himself when he comes home and maybe you'll be able to come back some other time.'

William thanked her and gave her his phone number in case she changed her mind.

The next house he needed to visit was two miles away and up a small boreen. The yard was very small and the dwelling house was an old stone cottage. Getting out of his car, he walked towards the front door already opened. Two small toddlers were sitting on the floor in the hall playing with some colourful Lego. William pressed the bell but on hearing no sound he presumed it was broken. So instead he knocked twice with the knocker at the letterbox. The children looked up and one started to cry. William tried to smile at her but she just howled louder. Within seconds a young slim woman appeared from a doorway.

Picking the child up in her arms, she walked over to the door and inquired as to what William wanted. After explaining that he called to offer his help she quickly introduced herself and showed him into the sitting room.

The room was small with just a brown worn suite of furniture and a television set. Here and there were scattered small toys and clothes.

'Won't you sit down Father, you'll have to excuse the state of the place the kids make a dreadful mess.' Marie said as she cleared one of the chairs.

'Oh I understand, 'said William smiling,' I have four nephews and nieces myself but I think they are worse somehow. By the way is your husband in?'

'No Father, Bob's at work. He works on the buildin's so he won't be home 'til six.'

'Would he mind me visiting you?'

'He'd be more surprised than anythin' else. I was wondering Father would you mind if I rang me neighbour Bridge, I know she'd want to talk to you, 'cos her young lad was involved in all of this too. She only lives close by.'

Taking the piece of paper from his pocket, William checked it for a moment and then replied,

'Mrs. Reynolds...oh yes, well it so happens she's next on my list for a visit. If there's anything I can do to help her I will. But if you wouldn't mind Marie I'd rather speak to you alone.'

'Right then,' she said as she called her eldest daughter to take the children out to play.

'Oh Father,' she whispered as she shut the door tightly behind them,' I'm glad somebody has come. What we've been through is dreadful but to be ignored was worse. Since all this started we've felt totally abandoned by the Church.'

'I just hope there's something I can do to help,' said William sincerely.

'Oh but Father, 'continued Marie nervously,' We didn't know what to do. Fr. Ferris was our curate. He came here to our home, I trusted him with me kids. They got on so well, he was a man of God or so we thought.'

'Well,' said William sadly, 'Father Ferris has sinned.'

'What I don't understand,' said Marie confusedly, 'is how a priest could do such a dreadful thing?'

'Well you must never forget that priests are human beings who are striving to be holy. Remember the Last Supper in Jerusalem? Well a man specially chosen by Jesus as his disciple sat at the same table with Him. But he turned out to be a traitor. Now if such a thing can happen to Christ then I'm afraid the Church will not be spared.'

'Maybe so,' she said wringing her hands, 'but Daniel's my son is a bundle of nerves now. He wakes up screaming and sweating in the night and he's started wetting the bed too. I go in and clean him up and then I sit on the bed and just hold him. Oh he feels so small in my arms. He's my baby, Father. I kiss him and tell him everything is alright. Then after he falls asleep again, I get so angry with Ferris that I want to kill him. I walk around the house with the anger boilin' inside me for what that beast did. Daniel was so happy-go-lucky until all this happened and now he's gone all quiet. Oh Father he was an innocent child. Why did it happen to him?'

William thought for a moment and then spoke directly to her.

'If you really think about it, most people who suffer are innocent, they do nothing to deserve it. But suffering is never a punishment, terrible though it is, we actually grow in spiritual strength because of it. God is very close to us when we are suffering. No matter what nature it may be, it is a work that gains the greatest good results and sometimes even miracles.'

'But how do you know that?' asked Marie

'Because God chose suffering to save the world.'

'That's all very well, but I'm afraid that this will affect Daniel for the rest of his life. I've heard that he might grow up with no idea of how to form a loving relationship. That he might be queer or violent, or worse still, abuse his own kids later on. Already he is gone quiet in himself, he just mopes around the house all day.'

'If there's nobody to heal the pain in your boy's heart and mind,' William replied, 'he will continue to hide inside himself. By doing this he thinks he will not get hurt. It's only by taking every opportunity to talk to him that you can get him to come out of himself. It's the mother that makes the home, and you Marie, by your attitude, and patience will have a great influence on how your child gets over this. When Daniel grows up and finds a partner you must tell him to be totally honest with that person about what happened. Then, if she truly loves him they will find peace. We all carry with us abuses and suffering's of one kind or another into relationships, but that's all they are, baggage and baggage can be thrown away.'

'But Father,' said Marie as she started to cry, 'the worst of it all is, I know he feels terrible shame for what happened, how'll he ever get over that?"

William looked at her with great compassion.

He knew in his heart that if she could only understand what he was saying that she would find peace.

'Remember,' he said,' the good thief hanging on a cross beside Jesus? Well when he offered his prayer, it was to someone who had sunk to the very depths of shame. But it was in that shame that the good thief saw the face of God.'

'But Daniel feels guilty, he thinks it was all his fault.'

'Yes he would, and if you would allow me talk with him please, I may be able to help get rid of that feeling of guilt.'

'Oh I don't know,' she said hesitantly, 'he doesn't like to be alone with priests anymore.'

This remark hurt William more than she could ever know.

'Well you remain in the room with us,' he said thoughtfully, 'and that way he will feel more secure.'

After thinking for a moment Marie agreed and went to fetch the boy. William stood up and began looking at pictures of the family on happier occasions hanging on the walls. The children's carefree faces smiled back at him.

'Oh God,' he prayed, 'help me to give back the happiness that has been taken from these people.'

Then the door opened slowly. William sat quickly back in his chair.

A little boy of ten, coaxed gently by his mother, reluctantly walked into the room. William, not wanting to stand up and tower over him remained seated. Reaching out his hand towards the boy he smiled kindly as he said:

'Daniel I'm Father William, will you shake my hand?'

Standing between the priest and his Mother, Daniel twitched awkwardly as he stared at William with sheer terror in his eyes.

William in turn, kept his hand extended and looked tenderly at the angelic little boy. From his perfect head of black hair, to his beautiful sad brown eyes, to his thick long eyelashes blinking nervously to his small nose screwing up.

His red lips began contracting as if he was going to cry and he nervously pulled at the top of his little yellow and blue tracksuit. Then he shuffled uneasily in his runners. In that moment William remembered what Jesus had said;

'That it would be better for anyone who harms a little child to tie a rock around their neck and throw themselves into the sea, than to face the punishment He had in store for them.'

Looking at the innocent young boy, William only now really understood the exploitation by anybody of the trust given by a child. He thought about his own nieces and nephews. He remembered how they would run to him, sit on his knee, and hug him with great affection. When the boy eventually reached out his little hand, his touch was like a feather. William wished he could give him a hug to try and take away the hurt. But instead he said quietly,

'Why don't you and your mammy sit down Daniel,' and he motioned to the couch,' I'd like to talk to you.'

In the next few minutes he looked and spoke directly to the boy.

He tried to explain that everything that had happened was entirely and absolutely Father Ferris's fault. He asked him to believe that he was completely innocent of any part of it. He told him Father Ferris was being punished for his deeds and was in prison.

'Good,' shouted the little boy, stamping his feet,' I hate him, I hate him, he hurt me.'

William was taken aback by this sudden outburst.

'Yes I know he hurt you,' said William, leaning over towards him, 'And I'm so sorry he did. But he will never hurt you again.

From now on if anyone tries to harm you, you must run away and tell your mammy or daddy, or a friend, or a policeman. There are so many good people who will not let anything happen to you, but you must tell them Daniel.'

'I wanted to tell them but Father Ferris...well... he said it was all my fault. He said I was to pray to God for forgiveness and I believed him.' said Daniel anxiously as he started to cry.

Marie put her arm around her son as William got up from the chair and crouched down beside him. Taking his handkerchief from his pocket, he offered it to the child and he was pleased when the boy took it.

'Well Father Ferris was wrong to say that,' William said quietly,' you must believe me when I say none of this was your fault.'

'I didn't know what to do.' the boy said, sniffling, 'I prayed for help...then I tried not to blame him, but then I...I just didn't know.'

'You tried not to blame him because you are a very good person, and that Daniel is very much like forgiving him. Now if you can forgive him you will recognize that he was the one that was wrong. You will feel a little better today, and as the days and years go by your forgiveness will become stronger and you will be free of this forever. Forgiveness is a quiet thing Daniel, and you must feel it inside in your heart. Only then will you know you have done it.'

'But Father never asked me to forgive him,' said the boy.

'He is too ashamed to ask you so I have come to ask for him instead. Always remember that good priests never do anything like Father Ferris did.'

'Yeah I know,' said Daniel positively.

Suddenly the boy relaxed and began to really listen to William.

'In the Bible when the little children wanted to come and talk to Jesus and the disciples said no, He was too tired?'

'Yes,' replied the boy as his eyes opened with interest.

'Well, some of those children were probably feeling sad like you are now. Jesus knew this and told His apostles to let the children come to Him. Then He sat and listened to what they wanted to tell Him. The reason He wanted to be with them was that He really loved them. Now when you're alone during the day take a little time to talk to Jesus. Tell him all your problems and He will listen to you too. Then soon you will get fed up telling all the bad things, and begin to tell Him all the good things that are happening to you as well.'

The boy gazed thoughtfully at William, and William hoped he was getting through to him.

That afternoon he stayed with the family longer than he had intended. Marie brought in some tea and sandwiches, and some chocolate biscuits and lemonade for Daniel. The boy sat quietly listening to the conversation. William could see from the corner of his eye, that he rarely took his eyes from his face. William wondered what was going through his young mind.

When the time came to leave he asked Marie if he could give them his blessing. She turned and asked Daniel if he would like that. The boy did not reply he just nodded. So Marie took her son's hand in hers and held it tightly.

Father William remained seated and raised his right hand over them. Then, after a few seconds of silence, he began his prayer,

'Jesus,' he said reverently,' ten lepers came up to you. Before they knew your love, they had the confidence in your power and asked to be made better. You did not inquire from where they had caught their affliction. You did not ask how they felt about it. You only saw that they were suffering and that you loved them. And so You healed them, and everything was as before.

Oh Jesus, look down now on this good and lovely family. Help them to see that your love and power can overshadow anything.

Then they might understand that every day is a new beginning.

We ask this prayer through Christ our Lord, Amen.'

William then blessed them both. As he went to leave, Marie told Daniel to go out and play with his sisters.

Like any other nine-year-old the child ran excitedly from the room.

Walking Father William towards the front door, his mother sighed deeply.

'All I want now is for Daniel to have a good life, and for all of us to have peace of mind,' she whispered hopefully.

He reassured her that she was not to feel alone or deserted in this. Then he wrote his address on a slip of paper and told her to write to him if she needed any help.

Taking the paper from him, Marie looked up into his wonderful sincere eyes and smiled:

'You know after listening to you Father, I think I could nearly forgive Ferris for what he done.'

William put his hand caringly on her shoulder:

'Well Marie,' he said hopefully,' anyone who could come out of such a thing, without feeling any hatred, would earn the respect of the angels for all time.'

CHAPTER 28.

With her head bowed slightly, a sad young girl boarded the B&I car ferry. Carrying a small bag, her slight figure went unnoticed as she moved along with the other passengers. Only when raising her eyes to confirm that she was heading the right way, did she meet strange gazes with an equally blank stare.

On reaching the restaurant she made straight for a seat in the furthest corner of the room. Sitting down, she pulled her unfamiliar headscarf a little over her forehead, then trembling she folded her arms tightly across her chest. She had taken to carrying out this comforting gesture quite a lot recently.

Feeling safe at last, she saw a young couple embrace and kiss lovingly beside the restaurant door. As she continued watching them, heavy tears filled her eyes and her own wounded heart rose up longingly in her chest. Then, together with all her dreams and wishes her thoughts were spirited swiftly across the room. In her imagination, she was the one in the boy's arms receiving all the caresses and kisses that he could give.

Reaching her hand up, she wiped away the intrusive tears now spilling out of her eyelids and clouding her vision. Suddenly the scene before her became unbearable to watch. Her sense of loss and isolation twisted painfully inside her. Standing up from her seat she had a sudden urge to get away. Blinded by more tears and followed by bewildered stares, she rushed past the embracing couple and out towards the privacy of the toilets. Hurrying into the first cubicle, she quickly locked the door.

Oblivious to where she was, she leaned against the wall and then slid slowly to the floor. Hugging her knees like a lost child she cried, moaned and sobbed until her throbbing head ached.

After a while the cold hardness of the floor began to hurt too, so rising up awkwardly, she wiped her eyes and opened the door. Walking towards the large mirror on the opposite wall, she was relieved to see the place unoccupied. But the face she saw reflected in it so unlike her own. Attempting to hide the dreadful turmoil she was in, she began to wet some tissue and carefully clean her tear-stained face.

Stepping out into the narrow corridor she found the movement of the ship only added to her unsteadiness and fatigue. Walking back slowly into the hustle and bustle of the now busy restaurant, she went unnoticed and returned to her seat. As she looked out of the porthole at the lights of Liverpool disappearing in the distance, the same words kept repeating over and over in her mind:

'I'm going home, thank God I'm going home.'

It was late the previous evening when Father William had received a surprise phone call asking him to meet her in Dublin early the following morning. As he hurried up the stairs in the main building he was surprised to see her coming towards him with a headscarf pulled forward on her face.

As he got nearer she rushed towards him and almost fell into his arms. He got it hard to keep his balance as he tried to hold on to her with one hand and the railings with the other.

'What is it Molly?' he asked worriedly as he felt her rigid tense body against his. But she did not reply.

Realising they were blocking the way of the other passengers he struggled to lead her to the bottom of the stairs.

'Let's get out of here and back to the car, have you any luggage?' he asked.

'No,' she said, shaking her head.

Once in the car he shut the door, walked round and got in beside her.

'Good God Molly what happened,' he asked as he took in the extent of her black eyes.

'He hit me,' she said quietly.

'Who hit you?' he said, reaching for her hand.

Her lips trembled. 'It was Edgar?' she said and started to cry.

Finding it hard to suppress the anger now rising inside him,

he reached over with his other hand to touch her head. But the movement of his hand was too quick, and the smooth shiny silk scarf slipped silently onto her shoulders. To his horror he saw that her beautiful familiar long hair had been cut off and in its place was jagged short black tufts.

'Did he do that too?' asked William in a shocked voice.

'No… I did,' she said as she pulled embarrassingly at the scarf and covered her head again.

'But why Molly, why would you do such a thing?'
With her eyes full of courage and her voice full of fire she said simply:
'Because sometimes it's necessary to sacrifice beauty for a life. Please take me home.'
As Father William battled his way through the morning traffic he thought it would be better to say little until he got her home. Suddenly he thought but where is her home? Did she mean his home, Riversdale House, David's home or Doireann's in Longford.
'Is it Riversdale you want to go to Molly?' he guessed carefully.
'Yes,' she answered in a quiet voice.
Trying to cheer her up, William told her how Frank and Biddy and little Francis had settled in and seemed to be very happy living there.
'I know, Doireann wrote,' she said looking out the car window completely unmoved by her Uncle's happiness. The rest of the journey was spent in total silence.
William knew that Molly needed the quiet to gather her thoughts, but there were a thousand questions he wanted to ask her.
When they arrived at the big house it was Biddy who saw them drive into the yard. But her excitement suddenly changed when she ran out to the car and saw Molly's face. As the two girls went into the house Frank said in a shocked voice:
'What happened to her Father?'
'I don't know, she won't talk.'
'Where did she come from?'
'Liverpool.'
'Why?... How?'
'Look Frank all I know is she rang me to meet her at the boat, she is very upset. Edgar seems to have beaten her and she has all her lovely hair cut off.' Then catching his elbow he whispered:
'Maybe we should leave her alone with Biddy for awhile.'
When they went into the kitchen Molly was sitting in Walter's old chair and Biddy was fussing and putting on the kettle. Fr. William walked over and pulled up a chair beside Molly.
'Molly I'm afraid I'm going to have to go but I'll be back up this evening. You get some rest you look all in, we'll talk later on.'
'I'll make up the bed in your room,' said Biddy smiling,' and if you like I'll bring the tea up to ya.'

Too tired to argue and too weary to care Molly agreed.

By the time Father William arrived back that evening Doireann had arrived from Longford. She was sitting quietly in the sitting room with Molly.

'Oh Father,' she said, rising from her chair to greet him, 'I'm glad you're here, this is awful,' she whispered.

Fr. William patted her shoulder reassuringly and went over to Molly. With great compassion he placed his hand tenderly on her small head. After the last few months of cold indifference and no affection, this small gesture was so powerful it broke through the icy frigid wall that Molly had protectively built around herself. Raising her head she looked up at her dear friend. Instead of the light of joy shining from her eyes, great tears welled up in their bruised orbits. An unfamiliar sadness had come over her face.

Brushing back her cropped hair he asked gently:

'Are you sure your all right?'

Composing herself a little, she dabbed at her tears with her hankerchief. Then she sat with her head bowed and began to tell how everything had gone wrong.

'I suppose it all started before Aunt Hattie and Uncle Walter died. Edgar had asked me to marry him, he even gave me an engagement ring, but when I saw how upset everyone was over Uncle Walter's death, I knew it was not the time to break my news, so I took off my ring and hid it. Then, the next day, Aunt Hattie died too and it was impossible for me to even think of my own happiness.

When I went back to England I was so lonely. The hospital seemed drab and depressing. It seemed like the whole world was sick or dying. When Edgar suggested that we get married straight away in a registry office and go to Spain for our honeymoon it sounded blissful. I felt so happy, it was as if a heavy cloud had suddenly lifted.'

'Why didn't you let us know Molly? 'asked Doireann curiously.

'I was afraid to tell you ...I thought you'd be upset with me for not having a church wedding.'

'Now Molly, we're your friends not your judges,' said William caringly.

Molly blew her nose and stared into the fireplace.

'Oh but it was so good in the beginning, we were so happy.

When we returned from our honeymoon, I set about decorating the house. Edgar said there was no need for me to work anymore, but I disagreed. So I continued my nursing, as I really wanted to finish and pass my exams. I spent my days off having long walks followed by hot baths and then cooking an evening meal. At first these evenings meals were just the two of us, but then his friends started calling.

They seemed really nice at first, one of them being an old school chum. It wasn't until later that I found out he was on drugs. Then we started meeting up with them in Hotels and restaurants. I didn't have much in common with them but I tried. I really did try to fit in and join in the conversations, but a lot of the time it was dirty jokes or double meaning stories. I smiled, but underneath I was squirming with embarrassment. His friends always teased Edgar about my looks and my long hair. He seemed to be so proud of me.'

'Well that's true,' said Doireann, 'you are beautiful Molly.'

'No, I don't want to be,' she said, turning away and clutching her arms tightly.

William signalled to Doireann to say nothing and let her continue.

'What happened then?' he asked.

'He started choosing my clothes for me, he wanted me to wear really tight short skimpy little things. I didn't want other men staring at me but he said I should do it to please him. He said he would look after me.'

'Did you wear them Molly?' asked Doireann

'Yes,' she said quietly, 'I wore them because I loved and wanted to please him. Then one night two couples came to the house and they brought a video with them. I knew there was something wrong because the others laughed like they did when telling those jokes. I sat watching with them, but as the film went on I felt a fear in the pit of my stomach. My true emotions seemed to ...just shut down. I continued watching but only with my eyes and not with my soul. I tried desperately to shut out what I was watching. But it was no use. So from a great distance I looked into hell itself.'

Her eyes darkened at this memory and she clasped her hand nervously to her lips.

'After they had gone home I couldn't sleep, the dreadful things I saw these people doing kept going round and round in my head. I couldn't shut them out. I tried to think of something good but again and again the images came back. Then the next day was worse. I went down to the shops but it was as if I was walking in a dream. My mind was still locked in the movie. Every man I saw became like the ones in the movie, capable of doing terrible things. Oh Father William it was like a great trust for the goodness of human beings went out of me and evil suspicions took its place.'

Noticing she was beginning to tremble again, William reached over and said concernedly:

'Would you like to take a little rest now Molly.'

Jumping up from her seat she said in a loud distressed voice:

'No, I can't sleep or rest until I tell you, I have to tell you, I need to empty myself and shake off what seems to be clinging to me.'

William rose from his seat, poured out a glass of water from the table, and handed it to her, while Doireann sat with her heart going out to her niece. Molly took a small sip and placed the glass on the floor beside her.

'From then on things got worse. I started finding pornographic magazines hidden under our mattress. When I asked him about this he just grinned and brought down some more from the attic. He said I shouldn't to be so small minded, that other women would find them arousing. Then he proceeded to show me the pictures of these women with no shame. As he turned the pages, I suddenly noticed a strange look coming into his eyes, almost like a starving man when he sees bread. I thought to myself 'I can't compete with the perfect bodies and seductive smiles of these celluloid women. They are not real only a fantasy...a lie. They do not care about my husband.' Then he started staying up late looking at more of those movies. I would lie in bed alone and I'd think to myself, what does he need me for if these things can arouse and satisfy him, the whole thing did not make sense to me.

One night we were in a restaurant... they all had rather a lot to drink. One of his friends Steven went to put his hands on my breasts and I instinctively put my hands up to stop him. When he sat back laughing in his seat I looked over at Edgar for help. But once again this evil grin was on his face and he said nothing. Later in the car park I told Edgar that I didn't like what his friend had done but he just said casually:

'You should have let him.'

When he opened the car door he began chatting to Steven. His friend then came over and got in beside me. At first I thought it was some kind of joke. As he started to drive out of the car park I asked him: 'Where's Edgar?'

'Don't worry about him Molly, he's quite happy,' he laughed, patting my knee. 'Now aren't you the lucky girl you get to come home with me.'

That now familiar feeling of panic came over me again.

'How do you mean?' I asked trying to stay calm.

'It's only a bit of fun, we're just going back to your house. Edgar will be there as soon as us.' But when we arrived at our house there was no other car. His friend laughed and said he must have got lost. Then, being real sure of himself, he took our car keys and walked towards our front door. I was so frightened, I was afraid to follow him into my own house. But when I did he had already helped himself to a drink and offered one to me. I said no and kept looking at the window for the lights of car the car Edgar was in.

'Suit yourself,' he said as he plonked down on the settee.

'By now I was really frightened. There was a stranger in my house and I didn't know what he was capable of doing. I desperately wanted him to leave. Suddenly my chest became tight and I started to wheeze. I reached into my bag and took a whiff of my inhaler. Then trying to stay calm I asked him what was going on.

'Look Molly, stop fooling around, you know the game, you know the way it works, Edgar is with Diane and you're with me.'

The smug grin on his face was just too much.

'Oh no I'm not,' I said, shocked at the suggestion.

'Look don't be so stupid. Once you do it the first time it gets easier, there is nothing bad going to happen my dear, it's just a bit of fun.'

He went to reach for me but all the months of hurt rose up inside me. By now it was as if the real Molly had become buried deep inside and an exterior one needed to defend her. So I lashed out and, God help me, I hit him.'

With tears in her eyes she said:

'I never hit anyone in my life before, it was terrible.'

With the tears rolling down her face she fell wearily to her knees. As she cried bitterly into her hands Doireann rose up from her seat to hug her.

Fr. William got up from his seat too, but for a different reason. He was hurt to the quick. Ashamed of the anger that was now building inside him, he walked over to the window and tried to hide it from the two women. Staring out into the darkness, visions of the night with Harold came back to haunt him. Then Edgar flashed through his mind. He shook his head in disbelief as he remembered the well - mannered young Englishman who had impressed him so much on their drive to Liverpool. He remembered sadly how pleased Roseanne had been when he finally found her estranged son. She had died happy just because she had met him.

Turning around, William now looked over at the sad sight of the two young women comforting each other on the floor. Once again he was witnessing the selfish cruelty that men inflict on the vulnerable hearts that love and trust them.

'Thank God Roseanne did not live to hear this,' he thought as a lump rose in his throat.

'Did that man hit you back?' asked Doireann.

'No, but he said, with venom in his voice as he was leaving, you will regret this.' Then he walked out the door.

'I stood in the room for what seemed forever. All the love and effort I'd put into it was now gone. Everything suddenly had a horrible feel to it. I went up to the bathroom and locked the door. It was the only room I felt safe in. I began hugging myself to try and stop myself trembling.

Then my breathing became worse. I knew I had left my inhaler downstairs and I started to panic because I would have to go back down to get it. I tried to breathe without the inhaler but soon I could hear my heart beating in my brain as my lungs strained to get some air down. Then I remembered there was one in a drawer in the bathroom. As I took a couple of big puffs, I will never forget the relief... I could breathe again. It was then that I caught sight of myself in the mirror. I remembered when dressing earlier that night, that I had thought I looked particularly well. But looking at my reflection my appearance seemed to me to be the cause of all the trouble. In that moment I hated what I saw. Without thinking I opened a drawer under the sink and took out a large scissors. Then I started cutting my hair off bit by bit. I was cryin' so much that I couldn't even see what I was doing."

Then, giving an embarrassed little laugh, she said regretfully: 'That's why it's all in chunks.'

Doireann stroked Molly's hair as the sobbing distraught young girl leaned her head over to be comforted.

'But what happened your face Molly?' asked William, returning to his seat determined to find out.

'It wasn't long until Edgar came home. I was in bed by then pretending to be asleep. He stormed up the stairs and dragged me out. I never saw him so angry. His dark eyes scowled as he bit his lip with temper. He began shaking me.

'You little bitch,' he shouted, 'how dare you humiliate me in front of my friends. You think you're so high and mighty. You walk into the pubs and clubs looking down your nose at my friends. You sit there, drinking tea, watching everything we do. Why you are not a real woman at all, that bloody Catholic Church has you sexually suppressed.'

Then, all of a sudden, he noticed my hair. The skin tightened on his face.

'What have you done?' he asked, grabbing it and pulling it roughly.

Even though he was hurting me and I was afraid of him, I got very angry.

'I've cut it all off,' I shouted back, 'I did it so your horrible friends would not leer at me with their lustful eyes.'

With that, a dreadful look came into his eyes, like I was challenging his authority. He lashed out and dealt a furious blow to my face. I staggered and fell to the floor. The blow was so strong it numbed me against the other painful ones that followed. I tried to pull away but he was stronger. So I just curled up into a ball and lay there. When he was finished he stood over me.

'You ungrateful slut,' he said, almost spitting at me,' I gave you a house, I gave you a car, I bought you expensive clothes and this is how you repay me.'

Then his fists tightened and I thought he was going to hit me again. I bent my head and covered it with my arms. This time I thought I'm going to die. But he just stormed out, went into the spare room and banged the door.'

William and Doireann looked over at each other in horror and disbelief. Then Molly continued:

'I lay on the floor, I don't know how long. My eyes began to swell up as much with crying as with the bruises I got. Then I felt so cold that I started wheezing again. I got up and having found my inhaler I took two more puffs and sat down on the bed. With my head pounding I started to put on my clothes. I was really afraid, I thought he would come back and kill me. I sat there trembling, listening to hear for any sound.

Then by four a.m. everything was quiet and I hoped he was asleep. By now I desperately wanted to get away, but strangely it was the hardest decision I ever had to make. I went over to the dressing table and took the few small things that meant anything to me and put them in a bag. I tiptoed out on to the landing with my heart beating so loud I felt sure he could hear it and I went even more carefully down the stairs. Then I hurried out into the dark, not even daring to shut the door behind me. There's a little hill outside our house and I free-wheeled my own car down it so I wouldn't wake him. Then I switched on the engine and headed for the hospital. I think I frightened the hell out of my friend Pat when she saw me. But she was great.

She got a friend of hers, a doctor, to examine me and as soon as she was off duty she took me home with her. The next day I rang you Father and...well you know the rest.'

When Molly finished speaking a stunned silence came over the room. Not knowing what to say Doireann got up off the floor and went out to make a pot of tea. William sat with his head bowed thinking deeply about all he had heard.

'You mustn't blame yourself for any of this Molly,' he said seriously,' it sounds like that man has some real problems.

Clutching her chest she replied with a desperate seriousness in her voice:

'No, you're wrong,' she said in a loud voice, 'don't you see...I am to blame. I was given a great start in life. I had people around me who cared enough to teach me what is good, honest and decent. I was so lonely and desperate to be loved that I disregarded what I had been taught and I put happiness first. Oh I deserve what I got because I was the one that let it happen. Bit by bit it crept into my life and I didn't have the wisdom to recognize it or the courage to stop it. I kept making excuses, he said he loved me and I thought his love would protect me. Even when I realised that he didn't need me because he was being satisfied by other means, still my stubborn pride kept me hoping he'd change.'

Taking her hand in his, William said quietly:

'Saying I love you is never enough Molly, if someone is not prepared to suffer things for you then that person will only use you. It's all over now and you must try and put it out of your mind.'

With a great coldness in her voice she looked at him and said:

'Oh no, I can never forget. I gave him everything that was precious to me. He took them and then he selfishly destroyed them. He humiliated me and took away my dignity. He mocked my religion and my background. He didn't want to mix with my family and he scorned me for trying to be good. He was so arrogant, he even thought he could swap me for the pleasure of other men.'

Then, getting up on her feet and with a terrible sense of loss in her voice, she said sadly:

'But worse of all, without giving it as much as a thought, he violated my innocence by forcing his unnatural desires into my mind.'

Chapter 29.

It was getting very late when Frank Thornton walked quietly into his sitting room. Seeing the tired strained faces looking up at him he suggested that maybe it would be better for everyone if they got a good nights sleep.

After thanking Father William and wishing him a safe journey home, the two girls climbed wearily up the wide wooden stairs.

'Would you like to sleep in my bed Molly?' suggested Doireann when they reached the landing.

Molly was glad to accept, as she really did not want to be on her own. Underneath the silk feather eiderdown the two girls snuggled warmly. They talked long into the early hours of the morning and, as they opened their hearts to one another an unexpected sisterly bond came between them.

As Molly relived again her disturbing time with Edgar, a sudden realisation came over Doireann. Then, without knowing why, she had an overwhelming need to confess to Molly the awful thing that had happened a long time ago now.

As she started crying, Molly sat up and said concernedly:

'Don't cry Doireann its all over now, I'll never go back to him.'

Through her heartfelt sobs Doireann said sadly:

'Oh you don't understand. in another way I'm as guilty of being just as cruel.'

'What do you mean?' said Molly sitting up in bed and leaning on her elbow.

'It was your mother,' she burst out.

'My mother!' said Molly in amazement.

'She was a lovely gentle person just like you, and I actually tried to hurt her.'

'But you didn't mean it, it was probably an accident,' said Molly hopefully. 'Oh but I did...you see...I was so jealous of her. She came down here, and she was so beautiful, so feminine, she was everything I ever wanted to be. I was jealous of the way everybody treated her like she was special. You see I was always a plain Jane, all I ever had was here in Riversdale. I thought that your parents would get married and come here to live. You see I didn't have anyone and I didn't have anywhere else to go.'

Turning around, she reached up and clutched Molly shoulders.

'I didn't mean it you know, I only wanted to frighten her.'

'But what did you do?' asked Molly, growing more curious.

Putting her hands up to her face, Doireann said ashamedly;

'I tried to run her down with my horse.'

'And did you hurt her?' asked Molly concernedly

'No, thank God I didn't, but something very strange happened. I remember it was a beautiful calm sunny day. She was walking towards Paradise and my temper was up. I went after her with my horse Pacha. As I caught up, I got it hard to hold Pacha and I guess I got a bit too close to her. Your mother panicked, she went to run away but she tripped and fell. Then suddenly a great strong wind came out of nowhere. Pacha, who was always a quiet old thing, sensed something, reared up and threw me to the ground. Then she raced off across the fields. I know there was...something...I can't explain what. When David rode up I tried to tell him what happened, but he just got angry with me so I ran home.

The following morning David told the Boss what happened. I tried to explain but the Boss wasn't having any of it. Since then I've tried to blot it out.'

'But you were mammy's bridesmaid,' said Molly lying back on the pillows.

'Oh yeah, after that I tried to make it up to her and for the short time I knew her we got very close. If only I had not been so influenced by fashion then, and went by my own instincts. I was happiest mucking about on the farm you know, but because of the media, I thought that if I didn't conform to what was the fashion of the day, a certain look, that I would never be happy. Thank goodness Garrett saw further than all that rubbish.'

A short silence followed Doireann's revelation and it was interrupted only by the sound of deep sighs and sniffling. She turned to Molly and said pleadingly;

'Come back to Longford with me. I want to help you through all this.'

'Oh could I? Would Garrett mind?'

'Not at all, he'd be delighted and you can get to know your little cousins.'

The two women hugged each other and a great affection and unfamiliar protectiveness came over Doireann towards the younger girl.

'This must be what it would have been like to have a sister,' she thought happily.

Suddenly Molly realised David would have to be told.

'There's something really worrying me, how am I going to tell Daddy?'

The next day, having promised his stubborn sister not to lose his temper, David fought hard to hide the dreadful anger which was raging inside him. Looking with sympathy at the pathetic sight of what was once his beautiful daughter, he listened without interrupting, while Molly told him about her secret marriage, and how she had been deeply hurt at the hands of a depraved little pervert. Swallowing hard he asked quietly:

'What would you like me to do?'

'Oh Daddy,' she said longingly, 'I just want to be free of him.'

'This marriage, was it in a registry office?'

'Yes,' she said, lowering her eyes.

'Well then there should be no problem, we will just get you a divorce.'

With a worried frown on her face, Doireann butt in:

'But he probably won't give her one.'

David jumped angrily to his feet.

'By God,' he said, with his eyes flashing,' if it's the last thing he does he'll give her one.'

'But how can you be so sure?'

'I will go and ask him,' he said firmly.

'Now write down his address for me?'

Molly went out of the room immediately to look for a pen and paper. Doireann rose to her feet and walked over to her brother.

'David, would you not get a solicitor on to this?' she whispered.

'No,' he said firmly,' these perverse little thugs have to be stopped. Somebody has to speak out for decent women. Why the Boss would turn in the grave if he thought somebody like that touched one of his. He would have torn their hearts out with his bare hands.'

'Yes but you can't go around doin' that anymore,its against the law.'

Running his hands through his long fringe, he said determinedly: 'I'm going to deal with this my way.'

Knowing how stubborn her brother was Doireann decided it would be better not to cross him. Putting her hand on his shoulder she said caringly: 'Just promise me you won't do anything stupid?'

'Of course not,' he said as he looked down and smiled at her.

Just then Molly came back into the room and handed him a piece of paper. Then she stretched out her left hand. She slipped off her shiny new rings and handed them to him.

'Daddy will you give them back to him.'

'Is there any message to go with them?'

Turning away sadly she said quietly:

'No there's nothing more to say.'

Crumbling them up in the paper, he shoved them into his pocket. Then he walked over and hugged her close to him.

'It'll be alright child, you'll see,' he promised.

On hearing the determination in his voice Doireann and Molly exchanged glances. In that moment they felt the Furlong's brave spirit was very close to them.

Chapter 30.

A week later when David Furlong walked quietly into the offices of Carlton Insurance Ltd. in Liverpool, he saw a rather painted up young woman sitting behind a white desk. Her long red fingernails and cheap perfume contradicted his first impression of her being a lady. As she in turn, saw this very well dressed attractive man coming towards her, her face lit up and she smiled in an extremely friendly way.

'May I help you sir?' she asked in a high squeaky voice.

'Yes, I want to see Mr. Archer please.'

Have you got an appointment sir?"

'No but I've come a long way and it's very important that I see him.'

'Oh I'm sorry sir but Mr. Archer is a busy man and he sees nobody without an appointment.'

Getting rather annoyed with her attitude, David took a deep breath and firmly repeated his urgency for seeing Mr. Archer.

'Well I don't know…'she said, as if between two minds. Sensing an opening, David made a suggestion.

'Why don't you pick up the phone and ask him if he would like to see me.'

The indecisive girl picked up the receiver and then inquired as to whom she should say was calling.

'Mr. Green,' said David smiling, 'John Green.'

As she listened to the angry voice on the other end of the phone, David could not help noticing her cheek colour changing to a deep red. Then, replacing the receiver, she picked up her pen and nervously looked down at a large book in front of her on the desk.

'That's fine Mr. Green, I will make an appointment for you now. When would it be convenient for you to see Mr. Archer, sometime this afternoon perhaps?'

By now David could almost sense the arrogant little man in the next room. Growing increasingly impatient he tried hard to keep calm.

'It is imperative that I speak with Mr. Archer now Miss, or otherwise I shall have to take my lucrative business elsewhere.'

'What is your business Mr. Green?' she asked curiously.

Thinking for a second David quickly replied, 'Gold,' as he fingered Molly's rings in his pocket.

'Just a moment,' she said getting up quickly from her desk, 'If you would take a seat please?'

David smiled as he walked over towards the leather chairs sitting neatly in a row. But being too impatient to sit down he just stood at the window and gazed at the traffic passing by outside.

After a few minutes the secretary reappeared from a room across the hall. Smiling broadly at David she told him most politely that Mr. Archer would be delighted to see him now.

Taking a deep breath, David walked with great strides towards the door. As he entered the small office, Edgar rose from his chair, finished buttoning his jacket, and held his hand out towards David.

'Mr. Green, I'm Edgar Archer, what can I…'

As David refrained from shaking his outstretched hand, suddenly the skin on Edgar's face tightened as a faint recognition crept in.

'I'm afraid your secretary got the name wrong, I'm David Furlong and I don't need an appointment.'

Composing himself quickly Edgar raised his chin up and in a flustered voice and said,

'Oh Mr. Furlong…how is Molly? I've been worried about her, where is she?'

'That's none of your business now,' replied David coldly.

'But she is my wife, I have a right to know.'

Taking the rings from his pocket, David took the engagement ring up first. Then looking Edgar straight in the eye, he crushed it between his thumb and finger. Doing the same with the wedding ring he threw them both down on to the desk.

'You have no wife,' he said angrily, 'Now I don't know what kind of laws you have in this country but you better get a divorce as quick as possible.'

Hesitating to pick up the rings, Edgar raised his voice in protest.

'Look Mr. Furlong, Molly and I are married, there is nothing you can do about it. She is my legally my wife.'

David moved forward and put his hands on the desk.

'No you're wrong there sonny,' he said seriously,' she's my daughter. Now I'm telling you, get a divorce or I'll kill you with my bare hands.'

Completely ignorant of the strength and determination of the Furlongs, Edgar drew a sharp breath in through his nostrils. Then walking defiantly around to the front of his desk, he stood face to face with David

Their angry eyes locked in a serious stare.

'Now Mr. Furlong there is no need to come in here threatening me like that, what happened…was a mistake. I am going to get my marriage back and you have no right to stand in my way.'

On hearing these words all the innocents who could not fight back against the likes of the scum that was now standing before him flashed into David's mind. The disgust he had always felt on hearing about women who had been degraded by his own sex, came into his heart and filled it with great repulsion. Then his anger exploded:

Taking Edgar roughly with his two fists, David grabbed the collar of his jacket.

'Don't you dare talk to me about rights,' he said with his face turning red with temper. 'The only rights you know is your right to take and keep on taking. Underneath your flashy suit and expensive aftershave you are rotten as manure. You're not fit to be called an animal. You and your kind have no place among decent people, for you are nothing but the scum of the earth and the leeches of mankind. Like snakes, you sneak into decent people's homes, and with your cunning smile you pretend to be friends. With your soft voices and your full wallets you tempt and seduce them. Wherever you go you find love and destroy it. But the lust in scum like you can never be satisfied.'

Looking a frightened Edgar up and down he continued speaking, his words almost spitting from him,

This outburst of sheer temper caused Edgar to stumble back down on to the desk, and he began to cough as the breath was slowly being choked out of him. Suddenly David realised the force that was locked in the strength of his own hands. Releasing the tight hold of his fists, he reluctantly let go and slowly straightened up. Taking a short step back he straightened his jacket and pointed angrily at the younger man struggling to get up.

'Oh no Edgar Archer,' he said, shaking his head, 'don't get me wrong, I'm not threatening you, I'm making you a sacred promise, not only for every decent man out there, but on the life of my only daughter. If you, or any one belongin' to you ever has any contact with Molly again, you will have me and to deal with. Now get that divorce and get it quick.'

Reaching into his pocket, he picked out a piece of paper and put in on the desk. As he turned for the door he said quietly:

'That is my address.'

Hurrying out of the office his eyes caught the confused look on the secretary's face. Then pulling his jacket and straightening his tie he said with a broad satisfied smile:

'I think your boss could do with a cup of tea now Miss.'

Chapter 31.

It was now two years and six months since Harold Ferris had started his prison sentence. In all that time he would not allow Fr. William or any of his own family visit him. Fr. William wrote time and time again asking him to change his mind but his plea fell on deaf ears. Instead, Harold sent a very short note asking for prayers for his soul.

So it was with great surprise that Fr. William received a second letter from the prison in the one year. On opening it he realized that it was not from Harold but from Fr. O'Reilly the prison chaplain.

He was shocked to read how Harold's health had declined and that he had suffered two mild strokes in the past few weeks. In the letter the chaplain told how the doctors held little hope of Harold surviving the winter. Then he asked Fr. William if he could come and visit Harold and preferably soon.

Two days later William was driving towards the Curragh Camp in County Kildare. His thoughts were occupied with memories of his old friend. As he drove out of the town of Newbridge a vast green space suddenly opened up before him. All around for miles stretched acres of flat short grasslands dotted with sheep, their thick wooly coats unnaturally streaked by red and blue dye. In the distance and right across the skyline stood many tall dense trees. As Fr. William drove onwards his car went up and down the little hills and hollows. Suddenly he braked as a horse and rider walked off the grass in front of him and started to cross the wide road. The sheep ignored them both and continued, with their little black heads down, they continued to graze contentedly. But William was charmed to see such a lovely sight. He could not help but admire the fitness of the horse, and the skill of the rider, Once they had both crossed the road safely the rider acknowledged Fr. William's courtesy with a friendly wave. Then they galloped off across the open plains.

Driving down the last straight stretch of road, the priest could see up ahead, a bell tower and another tall building standing high above the trees. As he drew nearer, more tall dark daunting trees surrounded him on either side. Suddenly he became aware that he was leaving the vast wide freedom of the Curragh behind.

A large notice at the side of the road informed him that he was now entering a restricted area where cameras or sketching were not allowed. Turning right at the large red brick church, he passed the fire station and continued down a long road. With a thirty mile per hour speed limit and lots of ramps, he drove quite slowly.

Looking left and right he saw old red brick houses and buildings on either side. Just past Connolly's barracks he stopped to admire a lovely small garden of remembrance. Winding the window down, he found the movement and sound of the waterfall brought life to the garden, while all around, carved in large pieces of granite stone, were the names of heroic dead soldiers.

Suddenly he was distracted as he saw tanks, jeeps and lorries coming towards him. Some of the soldiers greeted him as they passed by. William returned their greeting and then drove on. Coming to the end of the road, a strange errie feeling came over him.

Looking up he saw a large grey building which he knew by the high walls, topped with rolls of sharp barbed wire, surrounding it was the prison. Then he pulled into the car park and stopped the car. Looking up he noticed the lookout towers, the floodlights and the video camera's perched on high poles in the prison yard. Then he got out of his car, locked it and walked slowly towards the large steel gates.

A little later, accompanied by a friendly prison guard, William walked into a small cell. In a corner he saw a figure asleep in an iron bed. As he walked towards it the prison guard pulled a chair up behind him. After William thanked him, he tipped his cap turned, then left the cell and closed the bars behind him.

Alone now with Harold, the kind priest looked down at what was now only a shadow of his former friend. Harold's thin face had become a live canvas on which time had cruelly painted untold suffering. His high cheekbones protruded sharply through his pale transparent skin. His nose, unable to function properly as a result of the stroke, caused his dry mouth to remain open in an effort to breathe. Fr. William reached out and touched Harold's cold hand.

It was in this thin wasted body that he now tried desperately to recognise the healthy man who was his best friend. As he sat waiting for him to wake up Fr. William never once took his eyes from his face.

Just then he opened his eyes and looked disconcertedly at his visitor. With their brightness now dimmed somewhat, the empty eyes stared out blankly from their sunken dark sockets. This expression Fr. William found very disturbing, as it seemed to dominate his whole face and overshadow his other features.

Harold turned his head slowly and looked long and hard at William. Then recognizing his friend he reached over and put his other thin frail hand on top of William's.

'So they sent for you,' he said in a low voice, 'I told them not too.'

'Well I've wanted to come for such a long time, you know that, why didn't you let me?'

Lowering his eyes Harold replied:

'I was too ashamed to see anybody.'

'But what about your parents, do they know how sick you are?'

'No they don't...will you tell them, would you do that for me please?'

'Yes, of course I will, but I think you should let them visit. Especially your mother, she misses you and I know she's heartbroken.'

As Harold went to speak he suddenly took a fit of coughing. William rose up quickly, took the glass of water off the locker and held it for him. As he swallowed, his large Adam's apple moved sharply in his thin neck.

Then, he lay back exhausted on the pillows and William replaced the glass on the locker and resumed his seat.

'You see,' Harold went on to say,' I've denied myself the people I love most. Over the last few months I've walked up and down this cell thinking and thinking. I locked away the pain I caused those boys in my heart and I stayed silent.'

Tears began to fill his eyes as he squeezed William's hand, then he continued:

'You know, after all this time the relief of my soul is far from me,' then he whispered desperately:

'I think the devil has won.'

'You are not to talk like that,' said Fr. William worriedly.

'Ah but you don't understand how great my sin is. You don't realise how far I've fallen. But then how could you Willie, you were always so good.

'There is nobody good but God.'

'Yes,' agreed Harold thoughtfully, 'but you see I didn't know my limitations, I deserve no pity, you know I have even contemplated suicide.'

Shocked at this, William pulled his chair a little closer to the bed. Harold reached out slowly for his hand, then he looked deep into his friends eyes:

'I asked you once, a long time ago if you'd hear my confession, will you hear it now?' he begged in desperation.

Fr. William let go of his hand and sat back in the chair. All the emotions and especially his memory of his own behaviour the night Harold called for help came back to haunt him. Swallowing hard, he put his hand into his pocket. When he found his sacred stole, the feel of the cloth suddenly gave him courage and he knew he could never shrink from his duty as a priest and confessor.

Taking it from his pocket, he kissed the small embroidered cross reverently, then reached up to place it around his neck. Harold watched his every movement with the sadness of somebody who had lost something very precious.

Noticing this, William paused, then reached over and offered the stole for Harold to kiss. He leaned forward, hesitated and then turned his face away.

'No, I'm just not worthy,' he said sadly.

Lying back on the pillows, he looked up at the ceiling. Then, joining his shaking hands, in a choked and almost broken voice he began:

'Bless me father for I've committed the worst sin possible. I have betrayed God's love with my flesh.'

On hearing these words, William was cut to his heart.

'I've broken my sacred vows,' he continued, 'the devil knew how weak I was and he tempted me. I gave in to my corrupt nature. I used innocent children for my own sexual pleasure. I've brought terrible suffering and sorrow down on everyone. I know I deserve no forgiveness for I've even betrayed my Church. I am sick in my heart.'

He clutched his joined hands close to his breast.

'I was trusted by so many,' he continued with tears suddenly flowing down his cheeks, 'And I've failed them all. I've shaken the people's faith in the Catholic Church and in some cases I may have even destroyed it. But worst of all I've been so destructively selfish.'

'God,' he cried,' I'm so sorry.'

William looked painfully on. In all his years in the confessional he had never witnessed such agonizing regret. Every pore of Harold's body seemed to shake from unimaginable sorrow. It was so great that it forced more tears from his eyes and moans from his lips.

William, sat with his head bowed and his two hands clasped in his lap. He began to realise that Harold, in his state of sin, could only see the enormity of what he had done. He had completely forgotten God's unfathomable mercy and compassion. This troubled William.

'But are you truly sorry?' he asked again.

Harold looked up at his confessor with a troubled face. 'Am I sorry? '

With those words his body began to tremble again. He cried from the depths of his being. William was so upset by this that he reached out his hand to him again.

'Oh if only you knew. The light of grace has left me for so long and a dark emptiness has taken its place. I feel lower than a worm and as rotten as decay. I'd give everything I have to be able to turn the clock back. It's only now I know what I had, and it's only now I know what I've lost. There's nobody to comfort me among all those that loved me. All my friends have deserted me and I'm hated and despised by the whole country. To say sorry doesn't even begin to tell you how I feel. I'm eaten up with remorse and I shall never rest.'

Suddenly a shiver ran up William's spine and he felt cold. Evil had once more come between the two priests and he could almost sense the devil looking on in victory. It was now he realised the truth in the old saying: evil will flourish if good people do nothing. Then, looking down at Harold, he knew he would have to try and rise him up from the despair of his sin, and win his soul back for God.

Harold's weakness did not totally excuse him from what he did, but it did partially. So because of that, and being extremely moved by the scene in front of him, William asked God for forgiveness for the rest.

Then, with holy authority, he raised his right hand and in a strong voice full of mercy said:

'God forgives you Harry in the enormous depth of your sorrow, and He wants to restore peace to your soul. But I ask Him now, most earnestly to give you the power to forgive yourself. For your penance you must spend what's left of your life in constant prayer and sacrifice. You must give back to God more than you've taken from Him. If you cling to what has happened you will fall deeper into the despair of your own making. Don't look for human sympathy to comfort you in this, instead look to God. You must make it up to Him, Harry, that is the only way to live through this and come out a better person at the end.'

Harold looked up tearfully at William and said anxiously:

'But I'm so alone, God has deserted me.'

'No,' protested William, 'you must never think that or lose hope in the darkness that has come over you. When any of us are in sin it only appears that God withdraws, but He is always with us, watching how faithful and loyal we are. You know the more your flesh brings you down, the more God's grace will strengthen your spirit and raise you up.'

After thinking for a moment Harold shook his head slowly. 'I had forgotten,' he whispered.

Then, with a great effort he turned slowly, reached out with both hands and grabbed William's two arms tightly. Raising his thin frail body up a little from the bed he said in quiet desperation:

'But I'm afraid of dying.'

A wave of deep compassion swept over William as he looked down at his friend. Harold was like a little child with open fear showing in his frightened eyes. And in that touching moment, William was able to separate the enormous sin from the repentant sinner. Leaning over, he lowered Fr. Ferris back gently on the pillows.

'Harry,' he said tenderly, 'don't be afraid. Because of the way you have borne your suffering and realised the evil in your sin, I pray that your soul will take flight towards heaven. There, God, who is the fount of mercy and love will hopefully be waiting.'

As Fr. Ferris's began to believe again his eyes suddenly lit up with joy. Listening intently, it was not just these wonderful words of faith that lifted his spirit, but that when William spoke to him, the latter instantly recognised the old familiar tone returning to his friend's voice again. Then for the first time in many years a wave of inner peace went through him.

Letting out a deep sigh, he fell back on the pillows and looked up. Then with a voice full of sincerity he whispered:

'You know, while doing all the dreadful things that I did, I need you to understand that a part of me never stopped loving God.'

Chapter 32.

With the love and support she got from Doireann and Garrett, Molly's life began to settle down to a peaceful existence. She spent most of her time at 'Silverwood Stud,' playing with Doireann's children Doris and Jean. The two- and four -year olds crawled, clung, giggled, and played all over her. Their close physical contact and showering of unconditional love on Molly, brought back the familiar feelings of goodness that she thought were lost forever.

In turn, this stirred a need in her to get back to Liverpool and finish her nursing. It was so tempting to stay on in Ireland but, with her final exams coming up in seven months time, she knew that she would have to return.

As David left her to the boat the following Friday morning he asked worriedly:

'Are you sure you're up to this, do you really want to go back to England?'

'Oh yes Daddy,' she replied touching his arm, 'I love nursing and the Liverpool people are really kind. I miss my friends and I think I owe it to myself not to let what happened with Edgar stop me from qualifying as a nurse. Now don't worry, I'll be fine.'

David found that he had to admire her courage.

'Well if there's anything you want,' he said fondly,' you know you only have to ring me.'

However, once back in the now familiar City of Liverpool, she found memories of Edgar coming back to haunt her.

As she passed clubs and restaurants they had frequented, she recalled the conversations, the hurtful remarks and the sarcastic grins.

Pushing her hair back in a desperate attempt to brush away the memories, she bravely looked up again and kept her gaze firmly ahead.

Arriving at the hospital, her friends and classmates were delighted to have her back. As they sat chatting and giggling on her bed, they awkwardly avoided any reference to her marriage by telling her all that had happened in her absence. Trying hard to join in, she found she had to force herself to show any enthusiasm for their conversation. Deep down, her shattering experience had caused her to see life in a more mature way. Suddenly she felt a lot older and wiser than her friends.

However it was not long until she was back on the wards and in the swing of things. Working by day, and studying at night, she was glad to be busy as it kept her mind occupied. But often she would pause from her books and find her thoughts straying to those early days and happier times with Edgar. Her eyes would fill with tears, and pushing her books abruptly aside, she would cry into her arms. Then she would suddenly remember the bad times they had, and clenching her fists, she would cry out with the frustration of what might have been,

'Oh Edgar you stupid...stupid man.'

It was times like this that she would open her jewellery box and reach in for a piece of paper hidden in one of the compartments.

Then, reading it again, she would take great comfort in the words Fr. William had written for her.

Dispelling Darkness

Goodness is real, truth straightforward,
Honour and loyalty are their garments.
Should evil attack, it will first cause confusion.
The more confusion the more evil will get his foot in.
Soon evil and goodness will seem like friends.
Excuses are made why evil should stay.
Doubts creep in that you were never good in the first place.
Evil will cast a great shadow over everything and you will begin to feel dirty and unworthy of light.
Places of prayer are shunned for they become sickly sweet.
Places of darkness and noise are frequented to block out the small voice of hope trying to break through.
Soon all feelings of love and decency are numbed.
This progression can only be halted by taking a step backwards, not to when the evil started, but further back, to your childhood Molly.
Search there Molly and find those feelings of love, trust and innocence that you once knew.
Bring them to the surface.
If you feel nothing your effort alone will stir that little light buried deep inside you.
Everyday call to mind more of what you were before the darkness came.

> *Little by little evil will become too dark and you will find yourself letting in more light.*
> *It will be harder for him to cast his shadow and your light will shine so brightly it will blind him.*
> *Then once darkness is dispelled, your life will become an impenetrable fortress. Goodness, truth, and loyalty will stand with you and evil will limp away like a wounded animal.,*
> *Be gentle with yourself Molly,*
> *God bless ,*
> *Father William.*

At last the day of her final exam arrived. Having already passed the four practical ones on the wards, she hoped she was prepared to sit the written one. All the nurses compared mental notes and gave important advice to each other as they headed nervously towards the examination room.

The first paper of the morning was a multiple choice. Molly ticked the boxes she knew and then went back over the other ones, guessing frantically as she went.

After an hour's break for lunch the students returned for the longer handwritten exam. Having worked out a formula in her head for the general admitting of patients to hospital, she quickly wrote it down as soon as the supervisor told them to open their exam paper. Then, according as each different nursing question came up, she just checked her list and wrote down what was applicable to that particular case. For the first hour the hands of the clock went quite slowly, but after that whenever Molly checked the time it seemed to be flying. With her cheeks on fire from the pressure of her mind, she only stopped writing to straighten her stiff back.

The silence in the room hung almost as heavy as the stale air.

Eventually, when it was time to down pens, close papers and leave the examination hall. Out in the narrow passage the relieved nurses compared notes. At times Molly thought it might be better if nobody said anything, as some of nurses had a different answer to specific questions. This difference of opinion led some to believe they were wrong, and cast doubts in the minds of others who thought they had got it right. Eventually when they had dissected the papers to death they grew weary and unanimously decided to leave everything to fate. Then somebody made the best suggestion they had heard all day:

'Let's hit the town.'

With that, the quiet of Hill House Nurse's home was interrupted by loud music and excited girls rushing about. Then, with the pressure of the exam over, and the taxis ordered they headed into town to celebrate.

Two weeks later Molly boarded an Aer Lingus plane and flew back home.

Despite sincere pleas from her friends, she decided not to stay working in the hospital. Instead she asked her friend Pat to telephone home the minute her exam results arrived.

With word of her divorce coming through she was anxious to leave. But above everything she was really looking forward to seeing the children again.

'We're delighted to have you back,' said Garrett as he met her at the airport that night and relieved her of her large, heavy suitcase.

Having slept most of the way down in the car, she found it difficult to sleep when she eventually got to bed. So Molly lay thinking long and hard into the night.

For the first time in many months she began to think about her own needs. In a childlike way she now felt safe tucked up in bed in Doireann's house. But deep down Molly was no child. She was a full- bloodied woman. She had experienced the excitement of meeting somebody who fascinated her, the joy of falling in love, the giving of herself as she committed to a marriage, and then ultimately the pleasure of making love.

Lying in the double bed, she hugged her young curvaceous body as she thought yearningly:

'I have to find love again.'

Then with the loneliness welling up inside her she sobbed herself to sleep. The next morning she was up bright and early.

Opening the front door, the warmth of the spring sun streamed into the hall.

'It's such a beautiful day,' she thought happily.

The sky was a clear blue and little birds dived excitedly up and down and around the garden. Landing briefly on the fountain, they took all of a second to survey their surroundings, and then just as quickly they flew off again. Then, as if they could not waste a minute of life, they soared up into the heavens. As Molly closed the door again she smiled as if all that beauty was especially for her.

Walking into the kitchen she saw the back door open and the kettle was steaming on the cooker. Deciding to make herself a cup of tea, she chose a bright colourful mug, rather than a cup, from the dresser. Then, leaning on the door- post, she wrapped her cold hands around the warm mug and gratefully sipped the tea. The noise of hooves on the cobblestones rang out sharply in the air as she watched the horses being led in and out of the yard by Doireann and Garrett. With the whinnying of the other horses in the stables and the clanging of buckets, familiar memories of being in the big house with her late grandfather came flooding back to her.

As Doireann emerged from one of the stables the children trailing behind her let out an excited scream when they saw Molly. As they raced towards her she put her mug on the ground crouched, down on her hunkers and opened her arms.

Doris threw herself into them saying;

'You're back,' and clamping her two little arms around her neck, almost choked her with a hug. Over her shoulder Molly noticed that Sara had stopped in her tracks.

'Have you no hug for me Jean?' she asked with a mock frown on her forehead. The child pointed back to the yard,

'Daddy...work,' she said very seriously.

It was the first time Molly had heard the child speak, and a surge of love went right through her. Smiling she grabbed her little body and hugged her close.

Looking down at the three of them, Doireann said mischievously:

'I told ya I had a surprise for ya girls.'

After breakfast they took Molly by the hand and delighted in showing her around the farmyard. The little chickens, the calves, and the baby foals were first on their list.

That afternoon while the girls were napping, Molly went off exploring on her own. It was as if she was seeing the place for the first time. Everywhere she looked mares and foals trotted proudly by, while others grazed contentedly on the lush green grass. Walking down the road, Molly found the open green fields on either side were in complete contrast to the high concrete buildings of Liverpool. This gave her a great feeling of freedom.

Her feet took wings and, as if a great weight had been lifted from her, she felt her energy renewed. This incredible powerful feeling led her ultimately to believe that she could walk on forever.

But eventually she grew tired and stopped to rest under some large oak trees. Settling herself down between their large roots, she sat with her back to the rough bark and looked up at the green leaves rustling above. Between the branches the hot midday sun tried mischievously to play hide and seek with her, but not wanting to play, Molly just squinted her eyes and let it win.

As she sat soaking up the peace of the beautiful morning her fingers idly played in the thick dry clay. After a few moments her eyes began to take notice of what her fingers were doing. Then, as if prompted by an invisible teacher, she suddenly sat forward and clasped a fistful of the earth in her hand.

A faint forgotten voice could be heard just as clearly in her head.

'Look around ya child, look closely at God's earth. Bend down and take it in yer hands. Feel the life in the clay. The further folk go away from the it the more they are lost.'

'My God this is what Aggie was trying to tell me,' she said excitedly.

Looking out across the fields memories of her lovely childhood came flooding back, the walks in the woods, the flowers and the wildlife. In her mind's eye she could almost see the sincerity in Aggie's kind face. It was only now Molly realised that the old lady had instilled in her a real love of the land. The more she sat and remembered, the more heartfelt tears streamed down her face.

Then, with a great determination in her voice, her tears confirmed the sacredness of her words as she said with untold joy:

'I'm back, Thank God I'm home.'

Chapter 33.

Taking a great interest in the farm, Molly rose early every morning to help Garrett with the horses. She found this so fulfilling and satisfying that in her eagerness to learn she asked many questions.

Doireann and herself would regularly go riding together, sometimes cantering, or sometimes racing around the area. Whenever David came down and joined them at the weekends he really looked forward to it. At last he could share his passion for riding with the people he loved.

It was at these times while out riding that David would try and talk to his daughter about life.

'I can't lecture you Molly because I too married in haste,' he said regretfully,' Over the years Alishe and I tried but it just didn't work out. To marry the right person is much more important than you know. We have to be sure. Nobody can tell whose right for you.'

'I know Daddy,' she said sadly, with a faraway look in her eyes.

A regular visitor to Silverwood Stud was the dashing young Captain Dane Fitzgearld. Hailing from the County of Louth, he was the youngest son of a small farmer. A tall, quite man who, together with dedication to his sport, and his gentlemanly ways, seemed unaffected by the physical beauty of his muscular body.

His face was not bestowed with the handsome classic features of a film star but it was an interesting face that one could explore forever. His lovely black fringe lay rather untidily across his wide strong forehead, while his kind twinkling blue eyes looked out intelligently from beneath heavy eyebrows. His nose was long and his lips were pleasing. When he spoke, the sincerity in his deep unassuming voice drew the listener's attention to his conversation and held it there.

A member of the army riding corps, Dane had travelled with Garrett to various competitions all over the world. However, in the last year he seemed to spend a lot of his time at the stud farm in Longford and even stayed over when he was on leave.

Doireann liked Dane and the O'Loughlin's spent many an enjoyable evening with a good meal and a bottle of wine listening to his adventures. Doireann appreciated all the help and invaluable advice he gave them about horses. But in all the time she had known him she could not recall him mentioning any special relationship or showing any interest in women.

So it was with a great quiet enthusiasm that she set about changing all that and cunningly planned to introduce him to Molly.

Rushing into the kitchen one morning she said urgently:

'Molly I need you to come and hold one of the horses.'

Molly immediately stopped playing with the children and hurried out behind her. As they walked towards the stables Doireann smiled excitedly to herself. Then hurrying into the stables, Molly was surprised to see a stranger walk out of one of the stalls. Doireann quickly introduced them and then she stood back.

She knew by Dane's sheer awkwardness that her plan had worked. He seemed completely bowled over by Molly's presence and beauty. So it was no surprise to her when later that evening Molly told Doireann that he had asked her out.

'It's not really a date,' she said, trying to disguise her excitement, 'we're just going for a drive.'

'Yeah right,' said Doireann, continuing to inspect the mare's foot as she stifled a smile.

Sitting beside Dane in the car, intrusive memories of Edgar kept surfacing in her mind. Trying to blot them out, a slight tension rose up in her head. Finding it difficult to relax, her hands kept fidgeting nervously with each other as she sat rigidly on her seat. Sensing this conflict of emotions, Dane reached over and took her small cold hand in his strong warm one.

Then he fixed his gaze back on the road again. As he began talking about his love of horses she listened and sneaked every opportunity to study him carefully. Although she was aware of an attraction between them, she shyly kept her gaze on his face. While discovering a wonderful manliness about him, she was aware that she did not know what he might be thinking. The sheer physical size of him she found frightening, as she thought about him ever hurting or abusing her. So protectively she decided it would be safer not to reveal the deepest parts of her personality.

But gazing sadly out at the countryside hurrying past, she thought that too it was a pity for she wanted him to know the loving carefree girl she was before her disastrous marriage.

However, as they journeyed on, he continued to hold and squeeze her hand. His reassuring touch and sincere voice caused a lovely feeling to come over her and despite her doubts and reservations, she found there was something about this man that made her feel safe. So for the first time since she got into the car she began to relax.

A few weeks later, taking a short break from a busy morning's work, Dane and Molly were sitting laughing on the bales of straw in the hay shed. Catching her unawares, he began to ask her about her marriage. Taking a deep breath, she began to tell him scanty details. But then the more questions he asked, the more emotional she became. Suddenly, to her embarrassment, she burst out crying.

His strong arms came around her as she just fell into the comforting warmth of his chest. Lying close to him, she went deeper into the darkness of her memory, images of the people she loved flashed before her eyes. The pain of losing Aggie, her grandfather, and Aunt Hattie, became entangled with the thoughts that had they known of her failed marriage, they would have been so disappointed with her.

While her heart tried to wrench itself free from these thoughts, Molly moaned, cried and clung tightly to Dane. Being very moved by her distress, he began to hold and stroke the back of her head, while the other one encircled her waist. In that moment he felt a great urge to protect her.

After a few minutes her tears dried up into short intervals of heavy sobbing. Suddenly she became aware of his closeness.

This both frightened and excited her all at the same time. But being starved of the affection of a man for so long, she continued to lie helplessly in his arms, he took her gently by the shoulders and held her back a little from him. Handing her his handkerchief he apologized most sincerely,

'I'm sorry Molly, I shouldn't have asked you, it's none of my business. I promise won't mention it again.'

'Oh no Dane, you don't need to apologise,' she said, taking the hankerchief and wiping her tears.

'Its not you... it's me. In the last few months I've talked more than I ever did in my whole life. The words just seem to tumble out and I can't stop them. It's as if they're still searching for someone to make sense of it all. Do you know what I mean? Sometimes I have to tell myself to stop going over and over it and let it go.'

Suddenly she had a great urge to tell him everything that had happened. She desperately needed him to know. As she sat recalling the bad memories,

Dane took in her lovely face and hair. She looked like a child woman, so vulnerable and so beautiful. Unable to suppress his own feelings any more Dane took her in his arms. In mid sentence he silenced her sad words with a kiss. His lips came down gentle and warm as they explored hers.

'Forget him Molly, he's not worth it,' he whispered.

Suddenly she became swept up into a forgotten world of love and desire. Putting her sadness behind her, she kissed him back just as passionately. Then a slight awkwardness came over Dane and he did not know whether he should stop or not. Molly looked up into his big innocent face and put her two hands up to his cheeks,

'Oh you're a lovely man,' she said sincerely, and in uttering those heartfelt words she brought back all the trust she had lost in his kind.

He drew back shyly and folded his arms.

'I'm sorry, I hope you don't think I'm too forward or anything.'

'Oh no Dane,' she said, with her eyes full of joy, 'I think you're lovely.'

Later that evening Molly sat in the warm kitchen with Doireann and Garrett. Enjoying a coffee after their dinner, she began telling them about her day. When she casually mentioned Dane, Doireann suddenly noticed that the bright light of life had come back in her eyes.

'Molly Furlong you're in love,' she said accusingly. Molly got so red that she could feel her cheeks burning.

'I am not,' she said, trying to look away from their teasing, smiling stares.

'Oh yes you are,' said Garrett, shaking his finger at her.

In the silence that followed a funny surge of excitement rose up inside Molly. Tossing her head back she got up from her seat, and with a carefree laugh that had not been heard for months, excused herself and went upstairs to her room. Garrett and Doireann exchanged great smiles as they watched her go.

Sitting on her bed, she went over and over everything that Dane and she had done and said in the last two months. The more time she had spent with him the more her heart had softened. Suddenly the realisation that Doireann and Garrett were right hit her.

Then, clasping her hands to her face, she let out a little laugh as she said with great joy:

'I do love him.'

Later, when she heard Dane's car driving into the yard she raced down the stairs and out to meet him. Her face was flushed and her eyes were sparkling as she raced up to him. Full of excitement she stopped suddenly not knowing what to say. Looking down at her flushed face Dane said in sincere amazement

'My my but you are beautiful.'

Molly reached up and instinctively threw her arms around him.

Hugging her back he whispered passionately:

'You know I love you, don't you?'

But she could not reply. All she could do was cling to him as her happy heart soared. Wrapped in the safe strong embrace of his arms, they hugged and hugged one another as if they were on a merry-go-round.

Everything she ever went through with Edgar became insignificant and seemed to disappear far into the past. All that mattered now was the pure love she was feeling for the wonderful Captain Dane Fitzgearld.

Chapter 34.

On the first anniversary of his mothers death Father William, carrying a large colourful bunch of flowers, picked his way carefully through Glasneven cemetery. He thought it ironic that after all he had been through in the last couple of years he had ended up being transferred back to Dublin.

'Well you won't need to keep an eye on my soul anyway,' said Seamus in his usual cheeky, smug way.

William smiled as he recalled his brother's words when he telephoned and told him the good news. Then, bending forward, he reverently and lovingly placed the gift he had carefully chosen on his parent's grave. After recalling the faint few happy memories he had of his father, and reliving again the many colourful ones he had of his mother, he said a short meaningful prayer and walked away-sadly .

In one way he was glad of the challenge of the new parish, but in another he knew his health was not what it used to be. Twenty- five years ago his energy knew no bounds, as he committed and threw himself into projects and fundraising. They were good years then, but now he knew he would not swap all that youth and enthusiasm for the peace and real meaning of life that he had found.

As he walked among the tidy graves towards the cemetery gate, he shook his head in disbelief as he thought of how proud and arrogant he had been in the past. Youth and strength had given him a false sense of security. He thought there was nothing he could not do, and nobody he could not help.

While all these ideals were good in themselves, looking back it now, it was his own lack of true humility and the fact that he had never suffered which had prevented him from benefiting from any of those experiences. As he sat back into his car he adjusted his seat back a little and sat thinking for a long time. So it was with a quiet strength that Fr William walked out on to the altar to say his last Mass for the people of Laois.

Having finished reading the Gospel of the day, he then closed the bible, bent down, and kissed it reverently,

Then he addressed the large congregation that had gathered to wish him farewell.

'This Sunday my dear people, I'm not going to talk about the sacred scriptures,' he began,' instead, I hope to remind you of the great love that should be burning in all our hearts and minds.

You may say to yourselves, what can a priest know of love, or life? He does not have the pleasure of a wife or know about rearing children. He does not have the pressure of finding work or making ends meet.

But remember, each one of you has somewhere in the past taken sacred vows too. In Baptism they were said for you, in First Communion you accepted the presence of Jesus into your souls, in Confirmation you became soldiers of Christ. In your marriage's you committed yourselves to each other, and at the hour of death you will hopefully request the last rites.

So it is with this familiarity of faith in the commitments that you and I have made, and because I am your priest, that I humbly stand before you to speak.'

Then taking a step down he walked over to the centre of the aisle and stood in front of the altar.

'In the beginning,' he explained, 'there was God, an endless being of perfection and life. He expressed His thoughts in the word, and that Word became flesh in the form of his son Jesus. Then from these two infinite beings, came a divine love, the Holy Spirit.

The love of this Holy Trinity is what our Christian lives are built around.

Our souls are formed from it and into us God has breathed life.

Why then I ask, do we fool ourselves into believing that we are the masters of the earth. Why do we live as if we are answerable only to yourselves?

Daily lips become twisted and ugly from cursing, mouths speak idle vicious gossip against our neighbours, and greedy hands reach out to steal.

Afraid of the power of silence we constantly shatter our peace with noise.

In striving to give our children everything we foolishly give them nothing.

We chase selfish pleasures while the people who love us are left alone. In immoral pursuits of every kind, so much monetary commitment is given, that directed in other ways, could heal so many lives.

And while respectfully we leave the old to keep the faith, we laugh at their beliefs and drive proudly away.'

Then he paused and looked slowly around at the staring faces before him. Raising his voice a little he said angrily,

'But it is when our own flesh and kind are abused that I lower my head and tremble in shame. Everything else pales into insignificance when I witness the untold suffering inflicted on each other daily.

In our shops and homes pornography has seeped in like a poisonous mist. Everywhere the dignity of men and women are violated. From this, a hardness of heart grows and kills all caring. We ogle naked bodies as objects and in our ignorance we forget that through them we were born.

Innocent children are abused, and if they are lucky to escape, they are left broken and confused. Hatred violence and murder result and man buries his fellow man in the ground.

Then bowing his head he said with great sadness

'And when did we do all this you might ask?'

Then, looking up again, he raised his voice even louder:

'We are all guilty by our silence.'

At these words Father William paused and a deafening quiet came over the congregation. Then, to the people whose souls were entrusted into his care, he said seriously:

'We, creatures made in the image of God, are afraid to speak out.

We, who were paid for by the death of Jesus, will not speak out.

We, who are temples of the Holy Spirit, could not be bothered to speak out.

I ask you all now in the presence of almighty God: Where is our bravery? Where is our gratitude?

Don't we realise we are only a heart beat away from dying and meeting our Creator?'

Then, turning back slowly, William walked back up the step.

Placing his hands on either side of the marble top he continued in a prayerful voice:

'Of our own we are not strong enough, we must pray constantly,

For women and children in sexual slavery, Lord help us to speak out.

For the sick, the lonely, the hungry, and the oppressed, Lord help us to speak out.

And lastly, for us religious who neglect our vocations, pray to the Lord to give us the courage to speak out.

Today we pray most earnestly to Our Father in Heaven to help protect the goodness in our lives. For as Jesus Christ, the way, the truth and the life, says:

'When you did it to the least of these my brothers, you did it to me.'

Chapter 35.

A bright red Mercedes drove slowly into the front yard of Mount Benedict. Switching off the engine, the occupant smiled happily to himself as he listened to the last of the weather report. There would be a bright start to this special autumn day, but later towards evening, strong winds would sweep across the Irish countryside.

After struggling to get his large chubby frame out from behind the wheel, the driver straightened up quickly, chucked at his waistcoat, and bounded up the steps to the red hall door.

When it eventually opened a smiling Lady Gowne appeared with a wide, brimmed navy hat and matching suit.

'Oh my dear you can look quite stunning in full regalia,' said her delighted admirer.

'Why thank you Major Fennell,' she replied as she quickly pulled her gloves on. Then taking a closer look at his attire she smiled amusedly as her eyes took in his large round yellow waistcoat, polka dot dickey bow and cavalry twill beige trousers.

'Oh my God!' she thought trying to keep a straight face, 'I'll be the envy of every woman there.'

As the Major bowed slightly, extended his arm and offered it to her, she in turn graciously accepted. Then together they went arm in arm down the wide granite steps.

'Your carriage awaits Madam,' he said, opening the door for her.

Then, after making sure she was safely in, he shut it behind her and hurried around the back. Then once again, he huffed and puffed as he struggled to get in behind the steering wheel. Shutting the door he started up the engine, and reassuringly patted Lady Gowne on the knee. Then he said in his usual commanding way:

'Tally ho Maureen let's be off to this wedding.'

Meanwhile the excited happy buzz over in Riversdale House was in complete contrast to when Frank had found the silence unbearable. Half dressed children were running up and down the stairs, anxious mothers were trying to do and think of everything, and Frank was shouting last minute instructions down the phone to a helpful neighbour.

It was into this happy confusion that, a half an hour later, William walked quietly in through the open hall door. Eventually finding Doireann, he asked if it would be okay to see Molly.

Arriving at the bedroom, Doireann put her head around the door and whispered,

'Molly, Father William would like a word.'

When William walked through the door Doireann closed it quietly behind him. William gasped as he beheld the sight before his eyes.

Standing with her back to the window, and with the bright morning sun illuminating her, Molly was an absolute vision in white. His eyes travelled in amazement from the sheerness of her long delicate veil set off with a fairylike tiara, to the narrow silk bodice of her dress. Then they went down to the wide flowing folds of her tulle skirt and lastly to her white satin shoes. Never before had he been so stuck for words,

'Do you like it?' she asked with her eyes begging him to give the right answer.

'You are absolutely beautiful,' he said swallowing hard,' You look so much like your mother.'

In the silence that followed Molly became a little embarrassed so she walked over and sat down on the bed.

'Well I hope it's not unlucky for the priest to see the bride before the wedding,' she said laughing.

He went over and sat down beside her.

'I wanted to spend a few minutes with you before we get caught up in events of the day. I hope you find real happiness this time.'

Looking straight into his eyes she said with great belief:

'I know I will.' Then she looked shyly down at her hands.

'I never really thanked you for all you did for me.'

'That's alright Molly.'

'I'll never forget how I ran to you when my life was in bits. How you listened to me, and with your true words you helped me to cope and make sense of it all.'

Patting her hand affectionately, he reached into his pocket. 'I have something for you,' he said smiling.

With that, he took out a little bundle and passed it into her hands. When Molly unfolded the silk blue cloth she discovered a small delicate rosary beads.

'It's not new,' he said apologetically, 'it was mothers. Well to go back further, it was my grandmother Nora on my father's side. When they were living in Cape Town in South Africa, my grandfather had it made especially for her. The beads are actually real diamonds and the cross is solid gold.'

'Oh it's beautiful but I can't take this,' said Molly, looking closer at the sparkling stones.

'But I want you to. My mother carried it on her wedding day and then gave it to me for my ordination.'

Knowing how he felt about his late mother Molly said quickly: 'But are you sure?'

'Yes I am.'

Then, with a faint thoughtfulness flickering across his face, he reaffirmed his wishes.

'We would both want you to have it.'

So not allowing her to protest any further, he stood up, kissed her on the forehead and walked over to the door. Turning the handle, he suddenly looked back. Then with a smile on his face he said casually:

'I think there'll be a lot of happy souls smiling down on you today.'

When Molly eventually emerged from her bedroom a little while later, a type of peace had once more settled on the house. Everybody had left for the church and Pat her bridesmaid, with Doris and Jean the two little flower girls, were just driving down the avenue. Molly lifted her dress and walked carefully down the steps, then just as she reached the end, David stepped out from the sitting room.

His intense dreamlike stare immediately conveyed to Molly such a complete approval that she knew this was going to be the happiest day of her life.

Outside the hall door, a big black and grey wedding car complete with ribbons and flowers gleamed in the bright sunlight. Paddy, the bearded uniformed chauffeur, held the door open for them as he wished her good luck on her day.

As they drove through the little village excited neighbours came out of their houses to stand and wave their good wishes. As she passed happily by, Molly waved back her thanks. Then, as they neared the church, David took her hand in his and said reassuringly:

'Sometimes we find it hard to believe that God punishes the wicked, but everyone rejoices when He rewards the good.'

Driving into the churchyard, they both broke into laughter when they saw a worried Lady Gowne almost hunting Major Fennell down the red carpet and into the church.

As the strains of the Bridal March rang out from the organ, Doireann checked her two little daughters for the last time, then blowing Molly a kiss, she hurried inside to take her seat.

On her father's arm Molly began her long walk up the aisle. She did not take heed of all the smiling faces turning to look at her beauty nor did she see the fabulous arrangements of cut flowers on either side. Instead, her shining eyes were locked on to the lovely man standing up ahead at the altar, patiently waiting for her. As she drew nearer to him, he turned around and their eyes locked into a loving stare. Then her father took his daughters dainty hand, and placing it carefully on the groom's hand, he locked them both in a firm hold. In that moment David gave away not just his only daughter, but part of his heart. It was only then that the stare of love between the couple was broken as the bridegroom looked sincerely at David and whispered, thank you.'

Then, taking two little steps forward, the young couple stood nervously in front of the altar and William reassured them with a smile.

Throughout the beginning of the nuptial Mass, the sentiments of love were brought to a high level by the great voice of the soprano, as she mesmerized the wedding guests with the power of her talent. Then there was a pause.

'Before this couple become man and wife ,' Fr. William announced, 'the bride and groom wish to exchange their own thoughts to each other, so if you would all please be seated…'

With that the altar boy walked over and handed Molly a small sheet of paper on a gold plate.

Taking Dane's hand, she looked up at him with happiness spilling from her eyes and said tenderly:

'You have the statue of a great man,
You have the wisdom of a mature man,
You have the face of a working man,

You have the muscles of a physical man,
You have the eyes of a sensitive man,
You have the voice of a real man,
You have the manners of a gentleman,
You have the heart of a good man...
But your soul...Dane is that of my man.'

In turn Dane took her hands in his and, looking deep into her eyes, said his own words of love.

'Being close to you is like being in a beautiful garden.
When I leave you, I seem leave a golden circle.
When I'm away from you I long to get back to your magic and colour.
I am lost in your beauty
I sink in your love,
And I drown in your passion.

Then a serious silence came over the congregation as Fr. William asked,
'Do you, Molly Harriet Furlong,' a slight pause, then he continued,' take Dane Vivian Fitzgerald as your lawful husband? '
As Molly willingly said, 'I do,' she knew in her heart that this time love would be for ever.

Chapter 36.

Two hours later, when they arrived at the hotel, Mr. Birmingham, the photographer, found himself spoiled for choice as to where to take their photographs. The large Georgian House was set in picturesque grounds of green manicured lawns sloping down to a small lake. With two white swans floating in regal style on the clear water, and a backdrop of colourful shrubs and mature trees, he found he just could not get enough pictures.

After what seemed like hours, the bride and groom, with stiff faces from smiling, walked into the dining room. Father William said grace and everyone sat down to the wedding breakfast. With the perfection and care of a family-run business, each delicious course was presented beautifully. Then with the meal over, the wedding guests relaxed and sat back to enjoy the many witty and sincere speeches.

To the strains of 'Some Enchanted Evening.' Dane and Molly took to the floor. As he held his wife close in his arms everyone else disappeared. Once more they became lost in the world that was shining in each other's eyes.

Doireann, Garrett, Seamus, Eithne, Frank, Biddy, David and Pat were soon joining them, while Major Fennel looked over longingly at Lady Gowne already out dancing on the floor.

An hour later, with the wedding in full swing, David signalled to Dane then walked across the dance floor and took his daughter by the hand.

'I've just remembered,' he said, shouting over the noise of the band,' I never gave you my wedding present.'

'Oh that's okay,' said Molly as she kissed his cheek.

'Ah but its not,' he said smiling.

'Now I want you and Dane to slip away quietly for a little while.'

'But where are we going?' asked Molly looking a little puzzled at her husband as he joined them.

'It's only going to take an hour or so, they won't miss us,' Dane said as he looked back at their guests enjoying themselves.

Once outside the three of them made their way down the garden and out through a clearing into the paddock. It was then that Molly saw the helicopter sitting quietly on the ground.

'Are we going up in that?' she asked excitedly.

With that Dane swept Molly, wedding dress, veil and all up in his arms and, with the help of Alan, the pilot, they lifted her into the aircraft.

Then David stood alone watching the helicopter propeller's start up and rise like a large bird into the sky. In one single glance his daughter, as she waved back, conveyed to him the same look he saw on her mother's face all those years ago. Waving at them until they were out of sight, his eyes filled up with tears as his mind flashed back to his own wedding. He sadly thought how the happiness of that day had been ruined when Mick McCoy turned up. Then as he made his way slowly back to the Hotel he thought about his beloved deceased wife. Then he remembered a poem he had not thought of in a long time. How fitting the words would be again today, and you and I together love, forever we would be.'

… 'Then turning he made his way back to the hotel and with a great happiness filling his heart he continued:

Flying high up in the sky now Molly's excitement knew no bounds. Holding tightly to the hand of the man she loved, she was speechless as they flew over the beauty of the countryside. For the next few minutes the world seemed so small and yet so vast. Dane pointed out landmarks to her and they both kissed passionately as they flew over the parish church that they were married in just hours before.

'Now I'm going to have blindfold you now,' said Dane, taking a small cloth from his pocket.

'But why, I won't see anything,' she said disappointedly.

'Well actually the helicopter is not your only surprise, there's another waiting on the ground.'

Completely taken aback, and in the darkness of her blindfold Molly excitedly wondered what to expect. Then there was a slight thud as the helicopter landed safely on the ground.

'Can I take it off now?' she asked impatiently putting her hands up to her eyes.

'Ah ahh!.. don't you dare,' he said quickly.

Then, jumping out first, he helped her out of the aircraft. With the wind blowing her dress Molly held on tightly to his hand as they bowed their heads and walked clear of the revolving blades.

'I have to carry you the rest of the way,' he shouted above the noise of the propellers.

'Why?' she shouted back,

'Because you'll destroy your lovely dress and shoes.'

Not being able to see she asked curiously: 'Where are we Dane?'

'Now Mrs. Fitzgerald don't be so nosey,' he replied as he swept her up in his arms.

'You must have patience,' he said teasingly, as he adjusted her weight in his arms.

So with her wedding dress bundled up under her and a strong breeze blowing in her face Molly held on tightly to her veil.

Then, with the wind blowing stronger, Dane walked on and on. His bride giggled excitedly as she clung to him. Suddenly he stopped abruptly and put her carefully down on the ground. Molly could hear the rattling of keys as he unlocked a door.

Then, stepping back, he said protectively:

'Now darling be careful.'

Putting her arms out, Molly felt clumsily around with her hands as she stepped through a door.

Then, once inside, she could hear Dane switching on lights here, there and everywhere.

'Now you can look,' he said excitedly.

Quickly removing the blindfold she said: 'Where on earth are we?'

Pointing to a large picture hanging over the fireplace Dane said proudly,

'It's the cottage…Aggie's cottage.'

Molly put her two hands up to her shocked face and shaking her head, said in disbelief,

'Oh I don't believe it.'

With lights recessed into the white-washed ceiling, and scented candles everywhere, for the first time ever the kitchen seemed so bright. The fireplace was as Molly remembered and the turf burned brightly in the hearth.

Up above on the wall a photograph of Aggie had been enlarged and now hung in an expensive golden frame.

'Everything is so beautiful,' said Molly in amazement. Then, looking around the kitchen, she noticed on the ledges and on the table, bunches of flowers in new earthenware pottery, their wonderful fragrance filling the air. Up above on the wall a photograph of Aggie had been enlarged and now hung in an expensive golden frame. Beside the fireplace Aggie's dark chair had been lovingly restored.

Looking down at the old stone floor, Molly noticed the flagstones had been repaired, reset and highly polished.

Twirling around slowly, she asked: 'But when?... how?... who?'

'Sit down and let me explain everything,' said Dane taking her hand.

'No,' she said excitedly as she let it go, 'I have to look around.'

Then, racing into Aggie's old bedroom, she stood like a pilgrim to a shrine. The old bed and wardrobe were replaced with lovely new pine ones. On the locker was the picture of Aggie's soldier also in a beautiful new frame. Standing in the small room, Molly looked down at the big fluffy pillows under the new patchwork quilt. In her mind's eye she could almost see Aggie smiling at her from the bed. Tears filled her eyes as she held onto the bedpost. Coming up behind her, Dane put his arms lovingly around her.

After a few moments they walked back out from the bedroom and Molly went over to the other end of the kitchen. The dark settle bed was now re-upholstered in rich red leather. The old coats that had hung by the chimney breast were now gone, and in their place was a slim antique hall stand. Then Molly noticed a door that was not there before.

'What's out there?' she asked curiously.

'Out there my darling, you have a sitting room, two bathrooms and three extra big bedrooms.'

'I don't believe you,' said Molly as she went out quickly to see the extension for herself. Wandering from one room lovelier than the next, she then returned back to the kitchen moments later with her face all flushed and breathless.

Dane suggested that now she might sit down.

'I'm not going to tell you how this happened Molly, it's all in this letter,' he said handing her an envelope.

Walking across the floor, Molly removed her veil and carefully placed it on settle bed. Then, sitting down beside it she opened the sealed envelope and began to read:

'My darling Molly,
By the time you get this letter you will be Mrs. Dane Fitzgerald, and you should be standing in Aggies Cullen's cottage. It was your grandfather's wish that you should inherit this cottage, and, over the last few months, I had the pleasure of having it completely done up. Only a privileged few knew about this and were sworn to secrecy.
(However you gave us a few scares from time to time when you went on your walks.)

Molly smiled as she suddenly remembered those occasions. Then, clutching the gold locket around her neck she continued to read on:

'In keeping with the originality of the kitchen, and Aggie's bedroom, I tried very hard to protect the specialness of the place. I know you found a magic here as I too did long before you. It was here I brought your mother the first and only time she came to Wexford.
God knows it would be the perfect place to bring up my grandchildren.
Love forever, Daddy.'

As Molly gazed down at the letter she suddenly looked up, and through her tears she saw Dane holding a beautiful white and black kitten with a little pink ribbon around its neck.

'I was told by a reliable source,' he said, smiling 'that this would not be a real home without a cat.'

Molly put aside the letter and reached up to take the kitten in her arms.

'I will have to call it little Blackie, 'she said, holding its warm, furry, pulsating body close to her cheek.

'Oh Dane what can I say....I love you,' she said with tears in her eyes as she smiled up at him.

'Would you like to see your garden now my lady?' he said with a mock bow. Jumping up excitedly from the settle bed, Molly placed the little cat down on the seat. Hurrying to the door she could hear the strong gusts of wind banging against the window- panes. Then, on opening it, once more she was stopped in her tracks. In the dusk of the evening the floodlit garden glowed like a fairytale. All along the path night insects danced around the tall soft lights glowing in black iron lanterns. The old flower beds were gone and, in their place, a beautiful green velvety lawn was set off by little trees and shrubs planted all around.

With the strong wind blowing her beautiful wedding gown, Molly walked slowly over towards a fountain in the middle of the lawn. She listened, delighted, as she heard the movement of the water trickling from the pitcher of a little stone boy standing nymph-like in the centre.

Dane emerged from the cottage and called out to her:

'Molly, what about your veil?'

Removing a comb from the back of her head, she let her long hair fall free down beyond her shoulders. Then she shook out her beautiful tresses. Looking up at the sky as if embracing the whole world, she put her two arms up and in a moment of sheer ecstasy said confidently:

'I want the wind to play in my hair.'

The End.